The Last Generation of Women Who Cook

Kathy Johncox

For Yvonne
Hope you savor these stories
my friend ... Bon appétit!

2012   Kathy Johncox

The following stories have been previously published:

"Fennel," *Buffalo Spree Magazine*

"Sugar Cubes," *The New England Writers' Network*

ISBN-13: 978-1477476406

ISBN-10: 1477476407

These are works of fiction. Names, characters, places and happenings are the product of the author's imagination and any resemblance to actual persons, living or dead, or events or locations is entirely coincidental.

Photograph: Mark Benjamin

Cover Design: Elizabeth Berry, Touchpoints Creative

For our Norwegian mom, Mary Herman, whose love, inspiration and dedication to nurturing her family, always and in every way possible, truly made family stories and family meals the ties that bind.

Author's Note

Everyone has a story about food.

An elegant and unforgettable meal. A cooking debacle or a culinary tour de force. A favorite dinner with a favorite person or a horrible dinner with a favorite person. A dinner date that promises so much more. A cherished family recipe. The accidental ordering of something you wouldn't eat—not necessarily escargots, but something like that. And on and on.

These stories offer an opportunity to think of food in a different way—as something that has a meaning that you thought you knew, but that now evokes something else. Pasta equates with anger, soup with revenge, rice with doubt and so it goes.

Perhaps you will remember a story of your own. May it bring you joy.

Many, many thanks

To my husband for his love and support and for giving me the space all writers need.

To my family for their love, encouragement and support.

To my friends, best editors and fellow writers: Deborah Benjamin, Zena Collier, Gail Hosking, Martin Naparsteck and Marianne Zeitlin.

To my enthusiastic, always interested and patient friends: Patricia Campbell, Maureen Lynch-Bennett, Jorge Samper and Carol Wetherald.

To Peter Hixson—fellow writer, mentor, friend.

To all the other people—you know who you are—who have listened to me talk about this book and offered advice and encouragement.

The Last Generation of Women Who Cook

Contents

The Last Generation of Women Who Cook

A s always, the calm of the private beach is contagious. Sauntering down the boardwalk that curves from the condos to the bay, you feel yourself relax. It is the rhythmic lapping of the waves, you think, the first breath of sea air, the salty fragrance of the water that makes you feel lighter. Really, you know, as you step onto the sand, it is the excitement of being here with your family that lifts you up. Every year, you think about the oohs and aahs that your son Ryan used to make when he was small, and his fascination with those timeless horseshoe crabs suggesting a past world.

Yes, it is your family—your husband, son, sister, mother and the rest, impatient to get their feet wet, running knee deep into the water, then stopping, transfixed as always by the vastness of the two blues divided at the horizon, light blue for sky, deep blue for bay. The horseshoe crabs, those prehistoric throwbacks, are nearly gone now, victims of pollution in the Delaware Bay, but your family comes back every year. Family—along with its customs and traditions—endures.

Looking back toward the condo, you see movement on the deck. The others are arriving. You pull your baseball cap down more tightly over your curly brown hair. You jog across the sandy beach to the boardwalk and quickly walk back.

Even from the downstairs hallway of your elegant rental, you hear the lobster clacking on the glass table in the dining room upstairs. Ryan has created that sound ever since he was six years old, first with wonder, then with mischief, placing the lobster on the table, then crawling under the glass and lying on his back to see the underpinnings of the strange feast-to-be. And now twenty years later, he is under the table watching the underside of the lobster once again, but this time, Jenny is with him.

As you reach the top of the stairs, you hear giggling, then Ryan's deep laugh, then nothing.

"Hey, you two," you say. "Don't torture that thing to death. It has to be alive when you put it in the pot, you know."

"Mom! Jeez! Don't sneak around like that!" Ryan bellows. He sits up under the table, bumping his head, never seeming to have any idea how tall he is. He crawls out, rubbing his forehead. He grabs you in a hug.

"I couldn't—we couldn't—wait to get here." He reaches down to give a hand to the slender blonde woman struggling to get out from under the table while trying to keep the lobster from falling off without touching it.

"Ry, you've got to grab it," she says. "I can't touch things like this. Get it!" Her husky voice goes up a register with each sentence.

"Ryan, get that thing," you chime in.

"But I want to ..." he starts.

"Get it!" you and Jenny both scream. You and she smile at each other, then you exchange firm handshakes. You tell her how welcome she is and how much you have looked forward to this week together.

Noise on the stairs signals the rest of the vacationers

2

are arriving. Your mother, father, and your sister, Diane, and her husband, Bill, struggle up the stairs with their bags.

"Thank God, we're here," your mother says.

"Can't wait to hit the beach." That's Bill.

"Can't wait to meet Ryan's..." Diane begins, then stops as she sees Jenny and Ryan trying to cram the lobster into the bag.

"You can meet her in a minute, Di," Ryan calls from the kitchen. "Gotta put these guys away first."

You and Diane look at each other, she questioning, you shrugging.

Ryan pushes Jenny from the kitchen ahead of him and bows deeply as he says "Jenny, meet the family. Family, meet Jenny." In the flurry of greetings and hugs, you see your mother and sister assessing the young woman as a possible viable addition to the family.

"I see you've got the main course, Ry," Diane says, grabbing him around the waist and making lobster claw motions with her other hand.

"Sure enough," he replies, making one of his hands a claw as well, using it to muss her short brown-gray hair.

You watch them play as they do every year.

"Help me unload the car?" Diane's claw hand asks.

"Let's go," Ryan's claw says and the two of them clatter down the stairs.

Jenny moves to the wall of windows overlooking the bay.

She says, "It's great to be here. It's wonderful."

"We always have a great time here," you say.

You move next to her and point at the ferry in the distance. "Doesn't it look small out there? Wait until it comes inside the breakwater. It's huge then."

You wonder if Ryan would have joined you this

3

summer if Jenny hadn't been able to come. You are glad to meet this girl Ryan had told you he had met at a Mexican restaurant where she was working her way through the college they both attended. He said the sombrero and the peasant blouse did it for him, made him ask her out. They had so much in common, he'd said. She has a great sense of humor. You'll love her, he'd said.

Jenny is saying something but you weren't paying attention so you respond cordially. "We're glad to have you here," you say.

"Thank you," she says, smiling, "but I was asking what I should call you."

You are unprepared for this question, so direct and especially so soon in the visit. Not having many options, you clear your throat and say, "I guess Lynn would be fine."

She nods her head.

"Groceries. Groceries." Ryan grumbles, smiling, making it to the top of the stairs. "What's so important about food anyway?" He stops for effect and staggers the last few steps, pushing his shoulder-length dark hair back out of his face. The well-defined muscles in his arms relax as he plunks the bags on the counter.

"Now there's irony or something," Jenny says. "All you **do** is eat." She smiles and twists her hair behind her neck. She lets it all fall behind her as she sits down on a Breuer chair near the table. She's wearing denim shorts and her legs are lean and muscular, with the beginning of the tan that blondes get, that deepens daily when well tended. Definitely Ryan's type, one of several such girls that have paraded in and out of his young life.

You go into the kitchen to begin unpacking groceries when Diane steps up to whisper your thoughts out loud.

"So what's different about this one?" she says.

4

"Let's stop speculating and enjoy this week, okay?" you reply. You smile slightly at how she always cuts to the chase.

"I can if you can," Diane says over her shoulder. "Now—to the beach."

Everyone hurries down the stairs, you included, a rowdy group going down the boardwalk.

Ryan shows Jenny all his favorite spots, one arm around her, the other pointing to the rock where he cut his foot at age seven, the sand bar where he found hermit crabs, the approximate spot where he spied the body of the two-foot sand shark at age ten, right after seeing *Jaws*, right after you had assured him there were no sharks in these waters. Jenny seems to enjoy his stories as she puts her arm around his waist and pulls him to her.

Your mother and father look out over the water, shading their eyes to see their favorite evening fishing spot off the pier, and Diane and Bill head for the rocks, where they wait for the ferry to arrive. You look back at the condo to wave at Kevin, your husband, sitting on the deck with binoculars, just as you'd thought, watching them all in his own first-day ritual.

The history here is good.

When the water boils in the lobster pots, you dump a handful of salt into each and turn to the refrigerator for the lobster.

"What can I help with?" Jenny comes into the kitchen, all business and ready to work. When you say you need the lobster, Jenny gingerly grabs the bags from the refrigerator and says "Now what?"

"Dump them in and slam the tops on the pots. I'll set the timer." You turn to the counter as Jenny calls. "Ry, need you."

"We'll just dump them into the pots," you say. You look out into the living room and see Ryan slowly tearing himself away from the sports section of the local newspaper.

"We've got this, Ryan," you start to say.

But Jenny calls him again and he appears at the kitchen door. Holding a wiggling bag in each hand, Jenny wordlessly engages Ryan in her volunteer task. He grins, takes the bags and deftly pours one into each pot. She slams the cover on each and brushes her hands together, a task completed.

"We're a good team," Ryan comments.

"We are," Jenny adds. "You should see Ryan in the kitchen at the apartment."

Even from the other room, you feel Diane's antennae rising. Ryan, in the kitchen at the apartment? Ryan, who has a hard time opening a can? Ryan, who can barely boil water?

You cover the table with a plastic tablecloth as Ryan and Diane put the finishing touches on a luscious green salad. Standing by his side at the sink cleaning romaine and washing mushrooms, Diane teases him.

"Your majesty, when did food preparation stop being beneath you?" Diane says, as she passes Ryan more mushrooms to wash. "I can't seem to remember you and food ever relating like this."

"I'm not a very good cook," Jenny answers for him, her voice muffled by the cabinet she is peering into, her task to unearth a cruet for salad dressing. "When Ryan discovered that, he pitched in. Now, he's the man." Her voice, freed from the cabinet, came through loud and clear. At that, laughter pours from the living room where the rest of the family is sipping gin and tonics and listening to the kitchen repartee.

"No, really," Jenny pokes her head out the pass-through serving window to look at the others. "I'm impatient and I burn things. In the kitchen, I'm bad."

"No woman is bad in the kitchen, Jenny," your mother says. She chooses a seat at the table. "It's second nature. And even on the off chance it isn't, I always say if you can read, you can cook."

"Nice theory but sorry, Gram. She's bad," Ryan says. He's smirking as he puts the lobster platters on the table and sits down next to Jenny. "And I know she can read."

"Thanks for that vote of confidence, I think." Jenny says, laughing.

"Well, you said it. I was only agreeing. You don't like it when I disagree with you as I recall," Ryan answers, grunting as she elbows him in the ribs and hands him the cruet.

You chalk one up for your son's girlfriend. Ryan was poking fun at her and she gave it right back. No shrinking violet, this one.

Everyone finds a seat at the table and the next few minutes are filled with the sounds of lobster shells cracking. Jenny looks lost as she tries to mimic Ryan's expert technique.

"Like this," he says, exaggerating movements as he reaches his fork under the tail to pry the meat loose. Jenny tries but can't budge hers. "Take this," Ryan hands her his piece of lobster meat, then begins wrestling with hers.

You and Diane shoot each other a look.

Ryan notices. "What?"

"Nothing," you say, remembering how possessive he used to be about his lobster, knowing that something is different.

When dinner is over, you and Kevin draw the short

straw for dishes. The rest of the group adjourns to the deck.

"So?" Kevin asks, leaning against the sink.

"She's cute," you answer. You nudge him aside with your hip so you can scrape the plates.

"What else?" he asks.

"Could you please do something productive, not just stand there and grill me?"

"Now I know there's more." He grins.

"She's just his type, that's all. Ryan always falls for the same type."

"What do you mean falls for?" Kevin fills the sink with soapy water to wash the huge pans. Although Kevin is heavier now, and less muscular, you see that Ryan has the same profile and body build now that Kevin had when you first met him. Kevin's hair is shorter and has some gray but it is still mostly brown and straight. You watch his hands move competently through the cleaning routine, biceps tightening and loosening with the effort of scouring all the deep places in the pan.

Kevin would not have washed this pan twenty years ago. You would not have expected him to. It was right here at the beach in the early years when everyone took turns cooking and cleaning up on alternate nights that Kevin had first learned kitchen clean up. It was only fair, all of the women had contended, as they always prepared the food at home. Whose vacation was this anyway? Amid some grumbling, it eventually fell to different permutations of the family, teams of sisters, brothers-in-law, Grandma and Ryan, Grandpa and Diane, husbands and wives, all alternating meal planning and cooking and cleaning up, with the aid of a handful of straws. It had been hard for you, sitting in a chair on the deck, trying to relax while others worked. You sometimes sat there

8

silently cursing your grandmother for passing down her habits to your mother who had dutifully, although lovingly, imposed hers on her daughters, more on you, in fact, than Diane.

"You know, falls for," you say. "It's defined as a temporary infatuation that goes by the board after the newness of passion has run its course." You smile as Kevin stops scrubbing and stares at you.

"You must be drunk," he finally decides.

"I just had a Shakespearean moment," you say and then you both laugh. "Anyway, you know what I mean."

"It feels different this time," Kevin says. "More relaxed."

"Let's wait and see," you say.

You join the others on the deck, watching Ryan and Jenny walk along the beach in the dwindling light.

"What did you mean, wait and see?" Diane asks.

"You know. About Jenny."

"I think she's cool. Now, we do know she doesn't cook. But maybe that's not important to Ryan."

"Should it be?" your mother says.

"Mom," says Diane. "Tell me you don't see that as a necessary basic skill. You sure did when we were growing up."

"You've got to roll with the times. It's different now. People have so many other things to do."

You and Diane both stare at your seventy-six-year-old mother in astonishment.

"You didn't talk that way when I was growing up," Diane moans dramatically. "All those potatoes I wouldn't have had to peel, all the casseroles I wouldn't have had to make, all the pie crust lessons I could've lived without."

Your mother says firmly, "Diane, you're a fine cook and you got your start right next to me doing all those things you just made fun of. But, I'm not sure I'd do it that way again."

"Don't write off the value of young women knowing how to cook," you say.

"But now all that cooking seems like too much pressure. Too much stress," your mother says. She looks at you both.

They continue talking but you tune out. For all Jenny's good qualities, will she be willing and able to prepare special lasagna birthday dinners for Ryan, to bake chocolate chip cookies on a boring rainy day, to create chicken soup for the flu that Ryan seems to get every spring?

By midweek, the family has settled into a routine. Fend-for-yourself breakfasts on the deck start your leisurely days. You all watch as Ryan scrambles eggs for Jenny, cooks bacon for Jenny, squeezes fresh orange juice for Jenny. When whatever he is cooking is nearly ready, he hollers for her to come make the toast or cut the bagels, and she tears herself from the conversation or the view and goes to do her part. You also notice that she always cleans up and a person like that is a welcome addition.

But even so, is washing the dishes enough?

You can't let go of what you heard last night as Diane and Jenny were washing the dinner dishes.

"This family is pretty focused on cooking, isn't it?" Jenny had said.

"And eating," Diane had added, laughing. "We do get into it. It's fun."

"You know, when I was younger, my mom worked full time," Jenny said. "She cooked a few nights a week and

picked up dinner on her way home the rest of the time."
You know, pizza, fast food, that kind of thing. Mom was
so tired all the time that seeing her cook never looked like
fun to me."

"Sometimes at the end of the day, you just have to find
that extra energy," Diane said.

Jenny's response was thoughtful. "While Mom cooked,
I used to watch the news with my dad, do homework and
play with my baby sister. We would eat and I would clean
up. That was fine with me." Jenny shook her head. "I
remember watching her, the fatigue on her face from
hassling with work, then after work hustling to prepare
meals, then at the table late at night planning meals for the
next few days. Every time I saw her rise to someone else's
occasion, I vowed not me."

In the hot summer air, you had felt cold. You
remembered feeling used up by the demands of the day.
And, you remembered the occasions that you, like Jenny's
mother, had risen to—and still do.

The next day, you all make for the beach. Kevin and
Ryan stab beach umbrellas into the sand and arrange chairs
to take maximum advantage of the sun. You rub tanning
lotion on your arms and legs and sit back in the reclining
chair to bask. Your skin is youthful and your careful
tanning only improves the look. The not-too-conservative
red bathing suit was a smart purchase.

Ryan rubs lotion on Jenny, then she on him, with a
familiarity that it has taken you and Kevin many years to
achieve. You are getting used to the way they touch each
other, casually and often, the way they smile at each other
like they are all alone. Small trickles of sweat are making
their way down your face and, wiping the dampness from
your upper lip, you remember your first summer here,

11

yours and Kevin's, before Ryan, with only your parents and Diane to share this beach house. You remember how you had struggled to be inconspicuous in your desire, to appear more like friends than lovers, then to find some places to be alone. How while you were in graduate school, you had made sure Kevin had seen how you could cook his favorites, make him happy. These years later, the thought of your plan for his conquest makes your face burn from embarrassment, not from sun. And now those things, though no longer new, somehow bind you together still, a comfortable bond that you both accept.

"It's good how they are together," your mother says parking her beach chair next to yours.

"I guess."

But how can they be good, Mom, you want to shout. She doesn't care about the important things, all that you taught me.

"They complement each other, don't you think?" your mother tries again.

"I think you—we—should all stop making them into a couple. They're just friends."

"Oh, you're smarter than that, Lynnie."

"Sure, Mom," you say. You stand up. "I'm going up for some lemonade. Want anything?"

"No. But, just remember this. Different or, in our case, younger women can bring new customs and add richness to a family. They don't take away from it." Your mother shakes her head and goes back to her novel.

You start up the boardwalk to the condo. You feel yourself drifting into what Ryan would call a funk. Enough, you think. This is vacation. You need to enjoy each other, not niggle at each other.

You have talked yourself into a better mood by the time you get to the kitchen. You are preparing a container of lemonade when a wind surfer on the bay catches your eye out the huge picture window. As you crane your neck to watch, suddenly you see Ryan leap out of the water, prancing almost, and you can hear his howling all the way from there.

"They got me," he yells. "They got me."

You stand at alert. Down on the beach, Kevin and Jenny reach him at the same time. Jenny waves Kevin off, quickly getting under Ryan's arm, helping him toward the boardwalk. Ryan is favoring his right leg. Kevin yells up to you. "The jellies got him."

You try to remember what to do. Something about meat tenderizer. You always brought it when Ryan was younger in case jellyfish were in the bay. Maybe there is some in the kitchen cupboard. Ryan's expletives are loud, punctuated by a litany of "ow, ow, ow." You dash to look.

You hear Jenny calling. "Lynn, get the shaving cream in Ryan's suitcase."

"God damn it," Ryan hops up the stairs. "And I knew they were out there, too." His right leg has several angry-looking red tentacle marks wrapped around it.

You have the shaving cream ready and you are about to send Kevin to the store for meat tenderizer, but Jenny calmly says, "Come on, Ry, to the showers." She helps him into the bathroom, grabbing the shaving cream. "Get a kitchen knife. There's meat tenderizer in my suitcase. Hurry up."

You run to do as she says.

"Shit," Ryan says. "Feels like spikes running up my leg."

"It's the tentacles," Jenny grunts, pushing Ryan into the shower stall. "Run water on your leg until I get the stuff ready." She reaches for the knife you hold helplessly and shakes the shaving cream.

Ryan leans against the wall, eyes closed, gritting his teeth against the pain, the water aimed at his leg full force. "Doesn't help," he says.

Jenny lathers his leg with shaving cream and says quietly, "In a few seconds the menthol will numb it."

"That's better." Ryan seems to be relaxing. You understand now that his calm is related to her calm. She smiles at him and you understand that she already knows this about Ryan.

Jenny scrapes upward on Ryan's leg with the dull side of the kitchen knife.

"This should pull some of the stingers out," she says. "It should be stinging less."

"Feels a little better."

"Okay," she says. "Now we do the meat tenderizer."

She stands up, water dripping from her hair and bathing suit.

"How'd you know to do that?" Kevin asks.

"Ryan told me how painful it was when he got stung once. I just went online before we left for first aid ideas." She took the towel Kevin held out to her. "I know Ryan uses menthol shaving cream. This was my special purchase before we left home." She holds up the large bottle of meat tenderizer, grinning.

"You are Wonder Woman," Ryan chimes in from the shower, grinning weakly.

Jenny crouches and pretends to use Wonder Woman's famous power bracelets to ward off evil.

You all find her antics hilariously funny now that Ryan seems better. Diane pokes you.

It's late afternoon and you're enjoying your pre-dinner deck time. As you listen to the others tell first aid horror stories, you remember it is Ryan and Jenny's turn to do dinner. You begin to think what you will prepare, absolve them of the responsibility, after Ryan's afternoon trauma. You finish your gin and tonic and get up.

"Where are you going, Mom?" Ryan says from the chaise, his leg elevated.

"I thought I'd start dinner. You guys can take a turn tomorrow."

"Sit down," he says. "We're good. It's under control."

"It's all right," you say. "I'll make pasta and sauce. Maybe a quick strawberry shortcake for dessert." You open the sliding glass door to go in.

"Mom," Ryan says. "It's our turn. We'll take care of it."

"I'm taking orders for seafood at the crab shack," Jenny says, whipping a menu from her pocket. As she reads the selections, the others grow more and more enthusiastic.

"Clam dinner," both Diane and Kevin chime in.

"Crab cakes and hush puppies," your mother, father and Bill decide.

"We're having spicy shrimp," Jenny says, looking at you for your order. You hesitate, already smelling the browning of the onion and garlic, mixed with the tomatoes and tomato sauce and the deep red of the Chianti in shining wine glasses reflecting shimmering candlelight. Then you notice Ryan looking at you in an odd way. He is looking at you like Kevin does when he is critical of something you did, a decision you made. You don't like that look.

"Come on," Ryan says. "Just relax. Why should you knock yourself out all the time? Get the shrimp. You'll love it."

You feel yourself tense up. You don't want to feel like that. You reach up to rub your neck and take a deep breath. You nod your head and say "The shrimp sounds good." And then, "I can still make a quick shortcake for dessert."

15

"No," Ryan says emphatically, looking at Jenny. "It's ice cream, right, Jen?"

She nods enthusiastically and continues. "We're stopping at the Dairy Queen on the way back to pick up some soft chocolate almond ice cream. That should do it, right, gang?"

Everyone noisily agrees.

"Let's go, Ry," Jenny says, laughing. "Even Wonder Woman can't fend off this clamoring crowd."

Ryan steps gingerly on his leg, then proclaims it nearly back to normal. You all cheer. He puts his arms around Jenny and around you, hugging you both to him for a minute.

Dinner is delicious. You peel your shrimp and chat with the family. You realize you are actually appreciating the value of relaxation. You listen to your family, their witty conversation, their teasing. You sense their joy just being together in this moment. With a strange new satisfaction you realize that it would have been the same over spaghetti sauce that had simmered all day or over special oven-fried chicken prepared with low-fat oil and secret spices. You hear Ryan and Jenny tease each other good-naturedly over who will do dishes. You know there would have been neither discussion nor teasing about that in your younger life with Kevin. Jenny and others like her, you envy their species. Unaffected by the trappings of tradition, they will achieve in the world on their own terms. They will survive.

You need air.

"I'm going out for a short walk before dark," you say.

Inside you grab a can of soda and a beach chair and hurry down the boardwalk to the beach. You sit in the chair and lean forward, holding the cool can on the back of your neck. As you look up at the darkening sky and the stars glittering there, it becomes clear that you and others like you may be the last generation of women who cook. You are the dinosaurs of the kitchen, and like the horseshoe crab, you are trying to survive in the relentless glacial drip of fast food and time-saving, take-out dinners with a foreign flair.

In the past, you and others of your kind might have thought that there was no love in serving roast chicken fresh from the deli, no nurturing in dishing out a lump of instant mashed potatoes, or tenderness in breaking open pre-baked dinner rolls. But you know now that you and others of your kind must adapt.

You stare out over the dark blue bay until it meets the deep, deep blue of the sky disappearing on the horizon. You pop open the can and hold it high in the air.

"To the last of the dinosaurs," you say.

Spicy Beef Barbecue

I n the late afternoon on the wrap-around porch of the main house, Luke tried to get comfortable, but his shoulders ached from the ranch work he and the other guests were obliged to do to get the true flavor of the west. Hell, all the flavor he needed was in the golden bottle next to him, in the slabs of bacon presented at the crack of dawn every morning, in the Tex-Mex fare that spiced up the dinner hour before the evenings of compulsory interaction with strangers sharing this week at the dude ranch began.

He held the cold brew to his forehead and allowed himself to be wistful for a moment. If only Roni were with me, we could watch the sun set and then turn in, as they say out here. But then, he reminded himself, she's the reason you're here. She's the one who pushed you to take a break from creating computer software, obsessing on coding solutions, working late into the night on seemingly insolvable puzzles. A break from all the things you love.

"And she's not here," Luke muttered softly to himself, pushing her away mentally as she had done to him physically, telling him to leave, just for a while, just to get it all straight.

He stretched his legs out long, leaned his shoulders against the wooden porch chair, and cupped his hands behind his neck. He closed his dark brown eyes, trying to stop the stinging from the day's onslaught of prairie dust. He rubbed the sweat-dampened ends of his dark curly hair, just before he felt the familiar sharp pain in the muscle near his shoulder, the one most affected by the stress of hunching over a keyboard all day. That's where it was, all right, everything he worried about amassed right there in the pain that never could escape notice, no matter what he did, whether it was grocery shopping, or washing the car, or surfing the Net or sitting on the verandah on a dude ranch, or even making love.

He felt sure he was here because Roni had sensed his growing feelings of inadequacy, a mix of exhaustion and psychic impotence that eventually had become the real thing. He had been too tired for sex or anything that took that amount of energy, and his fatigue evolved into performance anxiety that, at age thirty-five, made popping the question to Roni a very disturbing issue. Finally, they had opted for some time apart.

No, actually Roni had opted for some time apart. But he had bought into it, agreeing after they had had five arguments about food in as many days, each one ending somehow in a reference to his lack of desire. During the fourth disagreement, he had contended that her nightly selection of a container from the freezer, the folding up one edge of the sealed cover, the tossing it into the microwave, and the throwing it on the table with a fork and a napkin, lacked a passion for food. She, in no uncertain terms, reminded him of what she saw as his lack of passion for other things, then started to nibble on her steaming hot dinner, neatly separated in three small compartments, no one food daring touch another.

Her relationship to food was as unpredictable as her relationship to anything else. She would slave over certain meals and came home with others bought at the upscale grocery. But inevitably when he craved a home-cooked meal, she was too tired. When she wanted to cook, she did, but she groaned and moaned about the effort she was expending and always, always involved him in the preparation.

Roni did have many positive qualities, Luke would tell himself often. She was neat and efficient and had a logical mind. She was attractive enough to make other men look at her and more attractive than anyone Luke had ever dated before. Too bad she was developing into an insolvable puzzle, one he wasn't sure he loved so much.

Then came the fifth argument.

"Could you take the meat out of the crockpot?" she had asked. There was an edge to her request and if he had not been thinking about the latest programming problem, he might have reacted to it.

"Sure, baby," he'd replied absently, lifting the chunk of well-done beef and putting it on a platter. Ready to go back to thinking about the computer problem, he heard her say "Could you get two forks and pull the meat apart please?" He dutifully did that and was ready once more to relax with his Chardonnay when she asked him to pour the bottled barbecue sauce over the beef and put it in a pan on simmer. At which point he said, "I'm a little busy thinking. Can't you just do that part?" Whereupon Roni said she was sick of doing EVERYTHING herself, "If you know what I mean," and stormed into the bedroom which was the last place he would follow her.

Later that night he heard her in the bedroom talking to someone on the phone and when she came out she suggested some time apart, just to clear her head.

Waking up from a snooze on this verandah near Butte, Montana, several thousand miles from Roni in Syracuse,

New York, Luke thought that the smell of beef barbecue had been in his dream. Only when the ranch hand rang the dinner bell did Luke realize food was actually cooking, food with a smell similar to the beef barbecue that had got him here in the first place. Surprised it was nearly sunset, he got up, tucking the shirt tails of his newly purchased denim shirt into his only slightly worn jeans, and led by the smell of the beef, hobbled around the corner in his new and not yet comfortable cowboy boots. By lantern light, he saw long tables decked with gingham picnic cloths welcoming guests and inviting them, in the sharing of food, to become friends. He saw the replica chuck wagon, gate open in the back, holding an old campstove with its flames licking at a huge cauldron of tantalizingly fragrant, spicy fare. A cowgirl stood on a stepping stool stirring the bubbling beef with more energy and enthusiasm than he had seen anyone do anything lately.

He thought a cowgirl because her well-worn jeans, her work boots, the pearl buttons in her shirt glinting in the flickering light, all made her at home right there in the realm of Annie Oakley and Calamity Jane. Luke watched her reach into the iron pot, scooping and scraping the beef barbecue, her body undulating toward the pot and then away, then leaning gracefully forward on the stool as she peered into the dark center.

Roni did not speak with her body as she prepared to heat the food she picked up at the local deli, food that someone else had cooked.

Wisps of the cowgirl's reddish hair fell casually from the ribbon holding it back and her western hat, kept around her neck by a leather strap, bobbed up and down on her back. Roni's dark hair was gelled to keep it in place, no matter what.

As the woman used her shoulder to wipe perspiration from her cheek, she winced but this motion was made with such economy that no one would even know, except Luke who had made that motion a million times in frustration in the midst of a difficult software development project. His shoulder ached for her.

"Come and git it," she called with authority and a western drawl. The twelve other people on the week's junket meandered toward the wagon, with their substantial margaritas. Luke carried his beer bottle. He was beginning to feel Roni had been right. This was what he had needed.

"Here. You dish it up like this," the cowgirl said. She demonstrated how to ladle the tender shredded beef and tangy sauce over fresh baked biscuits. She cajoled them into dunking their corn on the cob in a bucket of butter and tucked a wedge of watermelon on the edge of each of their plates. She used her bandanna to wipe her neck, damp with the effort of serving hot food on a steamy Montana night.

Roni did not perspire, wouldn't do anything that might cause it, even refused him on summer nights saying too sticky, too clammy, too much, just too much.

Luke waited his turn, then sauntered over to the table closest to the chuck wagon. The woman, satisfied that all were served, grabbed a plate and efficiently filled it with the smoking beef, and sat down next to Luke, plate heaped higher than his, and greeted every one at the table.

"You're gonna love this barbecue. Isn't a person doesn't rave about this meal. Some people even take my picture near the pot while I pretend I'm stirring. Imagine that." And she laughed so richly, so deeply that Luke wondered how he could hear it again. Her chambray shirt boasted a smear of barbecue sauce on the pocket over her left breast, which captivated him even as he tried not to stare.

"I'm Letty," she said. She extended her buttery hand to the folks around the table. Luke put down his corn and wiped his hand before telling her his name.

"Your name is Luke Dalton? Oh, right." She laughed her rich laugh again. "That's a well-known name around here. You have heard of the Dalton Brothers."

"In the movies. And I do have a brother but we're both law abidin' folk."

"The Daltons had reputations, you know. Lying, cheating, stealing, womanizing. Not exactly the type a girl would seek out for a long-term relationship."

She smiled and dug into her barbecue like cholesterol didn't matter and fat was a thing of the past, devouring her food voraciously, with gusto. Then Luke dug into his own meal, his eyes widening in surprise at the delicate flavor of the strongly scented meat, the delightfully blended tastes of the sweet, the sour and the hot and something exotic, piquant.

"This is great," Luke said.

"Told you. You Daltons don't take anything on faith, do you?" Her face was made bright by the campfire roaring in the fire pit between the chuck wagon and the main house.

"You made this for real? From scratch?" Luke persisted.

"It's what I do."

"Ever use a crockpot?"

"Heavens no." Then she laughed again.

They continued in silence, but for Luke her laugh echoed into the night. He heard sounds he had never heard at home: crickets chirping and small animals chattering as they burrowed in for the night, cozy yet wild, alert to the tiniest sound, to every potential threat. The horses whinnied softly in the paddock not far away, rustling hay

24

as they settled in to spend some dark hours getting ready for the light.

Letty was so companionable and friendly. Maybe she was paid to be that way by the Silver Stirrup Ranch, but then again maybe not. Her cooking skill and her delight in the beef barbecue were obvious. No picking through the shredded beef, no half-hearted attempt to eat less or wiser. Just honest enjoyment of that and, perhaps, everything else. Cozy yet wild.

"What?" she said.

"What?"

"Stop your staring at me and eat your food. I'm the least interesting of the two, believe me. I'm going for another biscuit. You on?" She stood waiting as he shook his head.

The others at the table had finished their dinner and were wandering around the grounds, not too far from the safety and light of the campfire.

Luke watched her choose a biscuit. It had been a while since he'd even felt like contemplating making a move on a girl and now that he was tempted, there was not enough time to plan and carefully rehearse as he so often did. Like the flow charts he created for his computer software, he was used to creating comments carefully calculated to elicit the next logical response.

She flipped her hair back over her shoulder as she sat down and dug into the remainder of her barbecue, dipping the biscuit aggressively into the mix and lifting it to perfectly shaped lips.

"I suppose you want to take my picture stirring the pot?" She looked up, smiling.

"Actually yes," Luke said, realizing that he did. He hoped he had said it suavely, not eagerly.

"You're joking."

"No, really," Luke leaned forward. "You are the perfect souvenir. If I want to remember anything from this day, I want it to be you, stirring the beef, your hair blowing, the little wet spot on your lip."

Here he couldn't help himself. He reached out and touched her lip before he could stop or she could stop him.

Then he dared look at her eyes, big and brown and wondering at his actions, now that he had touched that spot, a spot he had touched on no other, nor had wanted to.

And her eyes were not unwelcoming, in fact just the opposite. Like a colt, he thought, honest and innocent like a colt, holding nothing back.

"No one has ever done that before," she whispered. "That was so, so romantic. Are you a photographer? Are you a writer? Worse yet, are you married?" She let her words flow with little care into the space between them, bringing them closer.

"None of the above," he said, breathing deeply, breathing her in, just in case she chose this moment to disappear forever into the night.

They stared together into the campfire for a while. Then, with a sigh, Letty stood, saying she had to clean up. She hesitated, rubbing her fingers on the tablecloth, back and forth, back and forth like a child stalling for time. "But then maybe we could go look at the horses." She motioned to the darker area near the corral, away from the firelight.

"Let's go now," said Luke. "We can double team the clean up later."

"Good God, no. The guests can't clean up. I'll lose my job."

"Hey, I'm a Dalton, remember?" he said.

She laughed and said something about Daltons and scoundrels and womanizers that made him feel strong and illogical as they strolled toward the sounds of the horses. Elbow to elbow, they leaned against the fence and stared into the dark at the shadows of the horses, some eating, some nuzzling each other, some staging impromptu short races here and there.

They aren't ready to settle down, Luke thought. The more they frolicked, the more strongly he felt their power and freedom.

For the first time in nearly two long and difficult years, he put his arm around another woman and his neck didn't hurt as he did it. There was no logic to his action but even so, Letty turned toward him with kisses that didn't even start slowly but rampaged like a herd of careening mustangs, kisses that he returned so wildly that the two of them could barely stand. Letty's kisses were laced with sauce sweet and hot.

"My, my," she murmured. "It's that buffalo meat."

"That what?"

"Buffalo meat," she whispered, her mouth close to his ear. "Promise you won't tell. I always add a pound or two to the barbecue. Some people say it does something to them. Makes them frisky, you know, like colts."

"Like stallions," he said. Surrounded by the whinnying horses, the chirping night birds, the campfire flames reaching for the dark western sky, Luke tasted her—piquant, exotic, and above all, new.

Breakfast

The long butcher block table in the kitchen was only one third of the disaster. Jeanie wasn't in the kitchen, Jeanie was still in bed but she could picture it all. Cereal boxes tipped over, empty orange juice and milk cartons, oatmeal spills, crusts of toast left on chipped plates, the table would be crying for help. She could hear Bobby crying, too, sitting in the high chair, alone with the mess while his mother, Paula, was in the bathroom primping for her first period class at the high school. She was running the water trying to remove the acne medication from her fingers without getting the sleeves of her leather high school jacket too wet.

Debbie, his aunt, couldn't hear him either, headphones blaring the latest top ten tunes for her ears only, as she scurried about, late for the bus that would deliver her to the first day in her ninth grade homeroom. She stopped dead to carefully tuck her new poor boy sweater into her back-to-school skinny jeans, smoothing the ribbed cotton shirt over her chest, grown pleasingly large over the summer. She didn't want to take the bus today. She wanted a drop-off so people could see her. Someone would have to drive her.

"C.J., you've got to drive me," Debbie hollered.

"C.J.'s gone and so is Joey," said Paula.

Debbie uttered an expletive and slammed the bedroom door behind her. The back of the door held the full-length mirror that reflected the chaos of her room in living color.

"Why do those idiots always have to leave together?" she said.

"Duh, because they're twins and they do everything together?" Paula hissed. "Now if you hurry up, we can make the bus."

Minutes before, Jeanie knew the girls had blitzed through the kitchen like whirlwinds, boxes flying through the air, milk spilling on the counter, half-consumed cups of coffee left behind, Paula probably forgetting her baby in the panic of preparing once again for a first day at school.

Jeanie closed her eyes. Last year was a blur. Paula, a sophomore, had staved off morning sickness with soda crackers and pretzels for a while, hiding her secret by leaving early for school and staying late, until Debbie let it slip in a moment of thirteen-year-old premenstrual craziness. Then Paula had been defensive for a while, and nauseous, too, as she professed her intention to have the baby, considering no options, never mind that the father had no interest in anything. Then she grew big and angry, too big for school and too angry at the talk of her classmates as they whispered that they had known she was headed for trouble, and see, they were right. And then she had needed Jeanie to hold her hand and squeeze hard as Bobby pressed and pressed against her, hurting her as he made his way into their family circle.

He was cute for a while with his peach-fuzz blond hair and big blue eyes, a curiosity of tiny body parts. But he cried at the ungodliest hours and wanted to be fed all the time. And while no one said they had told her so, she knew they had. Jeanie and her husband, Ben, had insisted she should finish school, and while the prospect had seemed grim, it now gave her freedom for six hours each day, and a chance to be in high school with her friends again.

Bobby continued to cry, louder now over the noise of the sisters. So far he had lived through seven months of mornings, times too hectic for his infant sensibilities.

Jeanie lay in bed waiting for the house to be silent before she went down. The kids could get their own breakfast. Paula would take care of her son. The girls would make the bus. Everything would be taken care of once again, another day. Ben was in the shower, sweaty and energized from his morning exercise routine, probably ravenous as usual but used to fending for himself.

Damn. Was the baby still crying? Where was Paula anyway? When she was nine, Paula had been the most sensitive, understanding child, malleable, her personality yet to be fully sculpted by Jeanie and Ben, but showing some promise on its own. Her blonde hair was so sweet and her blue eyes so trusting and innocent still for several more years, but then she started dyeing her hair, wearing dark clothes, then black leather. Just a stage, Jeanie had thought, until Paula started hanging with boys in the dark of night. And then Bobby came, as helpless now as Jeanie had been to prevent him. If she closed her eyes, maybe someone would take a turn tending to him. Maybe Ben, as she heard the shower turn off, his familiar humming the only sound that let her know he was there. He worked out ferociously at every opportunity, but he always came back to the noise, the disarray, the comfort that Jeanie had created.

Ben had told her that her laid-back ways and ready smile reflected the generosity of her heart and spirit. Without ever saying the word, "whatever" had been her philosophy. Whatever happens, whatever you want, whatever you say, had been her response to everyone and

31

every situation for the early years of their marriage, for the growing up years of their children, until the announcement of Bobby. Until then, "whatever" had been acceptable, but Bobby's coming cast doubt on the value of that philosophy, quietly, at least in Jeanie's innermost heart.

Every morning as she stayed in bed waiting for someone else to begin their day with Bobby, Jeanie considered what could have been different. It was not with shame but wonder that she viewed her grandson. He's part of us, she would tell herself all day long as she played with him, fed him, read to him, took him outdoors just as she had her own children. He's part of us.

But for those moments in the early morning before she forced herself out of bed, he was a stranger demanding attention she wanted someone else to give.

"Bobby's crying," she murmured as the bathroom door opened. The humming stopped. Ben emerged, gleaming with water droplets still on his shoulders, a towel around his waist.

"Okay," he said and dropped the towel, trading it for sweatpants, letting it stay where it fell, dampening the carpet.

"Thanks, honey," she said. "I need a few minutes."

"I know," he said, leaving quietly and closing the bedroom door nearly all the way.

Her daughters continued to taunt each other as they left. She knew they would remember to tweak or kiss Bobby on their way out, just adding to his malaise.

She heard Ben cleaning away the rubble on the table, tossing empty things into the full garbage pail, pushing them down with his strong arms. Ben's arms had held them all so tightly, first Jeanie, every day in every room in their quiet years alone; then the twins during evenings consumed by colic; then Paula during angelic naps in church; lastly Debbie at the end of some days when Jeanie was too tired to touch one more child for one more minute.

"Hey, Bobby," she heard him say and the child, lifted into those arms, cooed and gurgled and felt protected like she still felt, but only lying in the quiet of this bed, in the white of the sheets with Ben's scent around her, hearing him come back up the stairs, his humming mixed with the small, now happy, sounds of their unexpected arrival.

Cinnamon Rolls

T he yeast was calling to her from the refrigerator again. Its tiny granulated voice made itself heard for the third time this week. Use me, use me now.

Okay, okay, later, she stalled, but she knew somehow it was now or never. Use me. He'll love it. He'll love you more. He'll love you again.

She leaned back in the kitchen chair until it creaked, until she felt the early Saturday sunshine on her shoulders, warming them along with the ends of her wet morning hair. She wound it absently around her fingers, catching a glimpse of a few of the graying strands she had spent so much to hide.

She wondered if it would be worth it to use the yeast now. The yeast added the fluffy softness to his favorite food—luscious, warm cinnamon rolls dripping with pecans and sugar glaze, exploding at their cinnamon seams with golden raisins lovingly boiled to a state of puffiness before she added them to the confection.

Even after their years together and all the water under the bridge, she felt happy when she remembered his face on that very first morning of cinnamon rolls. She remembered his pleasure in the rolls and in her.

She looked at the knobs on the oven, mentally turning them to the required setting. She glanced at the food processor dial, in her mind setting it on cut, the verb that described the mixing of the flour and butter. But she should only select that setting after the packet of yeast had found its way into the flour. She would lightly filter it through the old-fashioned sifter they had found together browsing in an antiques store.

She stood, wrapping her white terry cloth robe tighter, scuffing her feet more firmly into her slippers. She grabbed her dark, drying hair into a ponytail and rooted around in the junk drawer for a rubber band. She found one with a celery leaf stuck to it, flicked the leaf into the sink and wrapped the red rubber around her hair. All this she did slowly to avoid the yeast packet, which, once torn, would be a commitment. But momentum and curiosity drew her to the refrigerator. The magnetism of the silver packet led her to open the butter storage bin, to slide the envelope out and, out of habit, to scan the expiration date, which was still within reason, and then to rip on the dotted line.

Its sour fragrance was not welcome, was never welcome. It always astounded her that this ingredient contributed so much to cinnamon roll success. If you put that much sourness proportionately into a relationship, she thought, it would never end up sweet and hot and enticing.

She was reaching for the large red mixing bowl when the phone rang.

"How about tennis?" Marla's voice sang through the phone. "I know you have the day off. I'm ready."

"Tempting," she answered and hesitated for a moment. "But no thanks. Really, no," she said more firmly both to herself and to her friend's silence. "I've just made a commitment to cinnamon rolls."

"I think I understand that and if I don't, I'll pretend I do," her friend said.

She hung up and reached for the flour. She stood on tiptoe to poke the confectioner's sugar down from the top shelf. When the belt of her robe got stuck in the utensil drawer, she untied it and flung the robe to the floor. She reveled for a moment in her nearly naked coolness. She stood there in his boxer shorts only, reaching high for the baking powder, low for the cookie sheet, over here for the wire whisk, there for the cinnamon. She worked with delighted abandon, not stopping once to consider what the neighbors would see if they were to glance out their kitchen window into hers.

She worked quickly and from memory until she stopped for a moment to sip her cooling coffee. Reaching again for ingredients, she had lost her place. She would need the cookbook. But her hands were full of flour, her stomach spattered with egg white, and she wanted to rely less on the words in the cookbook, not more. This was ridiculous. After fifty-two cinnamon roll sessions multiplied by six years, an experienced cook—no, an experienced baker—should know what came next.

She remembered what had used to come next during the baking of the rolls. They had waited at the kitchen table together in bathrobes, enjoying the companionable reading of the newspaper, the unspoken refilling of the coffee cups. They occasionally looked up and savored the fragrance, the smiling, the touching of hands and mouths as they fed each other. All those things were now preempted by his over-time work. His yard work. His board charity work. His weekend job. Now she was often alone at the table in her bathrobe reading the newspaper, filling her own cup, licking the sugar and cinnamon from her own thumb and forefinger.

Maybe he would have forgotten something today, and return home to find her topless at the table licking the sugar glaze from her fingers. He would sit down for a minute, for some coffee, for some warm dough rolled in cinnamon and butter, wrapped in raisins. And he would not be shocked but energized by her outrageous behavior. He would take some time before he had to leave again to share pleasure the way they used to three thousand seven hundred and forty-four cinnamon rolls ago. That's fifty-two weeks times six years times a dozen rolls. That's three hundred and twelve shared hours of pleasure looking to be three hundred and thirteen.

She would feel silly sitting at the table that way. But he would love it. He would love her more. He would love her again.

Ah, yes. It was the milk that was next. She felt relief at the memory. It needed to be scalded. This was the old-fashioned way she knew, but the process resulted in the best, the sweetest, and the most moist dough, and if you are going to do something you should do it well. This was the advice her mother offered as the wedding dress had slipped over her shoulders and down over her just slightly pregnant abdomen. This advice had implied that marriage was something to be performed or accomplished. It said that you have some control over how you perform or accomplish it.

And she had really thought so, too. Even after the miscarriage, she had felt in her heart things would always be the same.

For a while it had been that way. He had been so sweet and caring, helping her through all that followed. On the Saturday mornings that followed, the rolls were created like clockwork, but babies were not.

As trying as it was always to make the perfect rolls, it was easier than trying to make any kind of baby. It was a job. Sex had become a full-time job to be completed not when the spirit moved you, but when the hormones dictated. Lord knows she'd tried with lingerie, perfume and oils, mood music and wine. But running home at noon if the time was right, or being met at the door when he came home from the office, or being awakened early by an alarm set for a necessary morning attempt had removed the expectant grin from his face, transformed it into a grimace, in fact.

But she never tired of trying. She held on to the thought of the tiny egg fertilized and growing inside her. It was a fantasy she indulged every time they made love, even after it had been reduced to hurrying to the bedroom after looking at the calendar and taking her temperature. She would feel the connection. She would feel a spark of life beginning. She would bask in that glorious moment and stretch it into four weeks of anticipation until it was obvious that once again she had been wrong.

It was not that he didn't love her, she thought. He had made it clear he was happy with her. He was happy to be just two, to adopt a child, to get a dog, anything to please her. But she had pushed away his suggestions every time. She held out for something they would create together.

The cinnamon rolls were admittedly a poor substitute, but they were things she could create reliably and give him lovingly. They involved a sacrifice of time and concentration of effort she was certain he appreciated; the same sacrifice and concentration that he offered her when he willingly participated in their oddly timed but necessary trysts.

For the first time, her shoulders ached and for the first time her wrists cracked from the kneading, reminding her that something needed to change. Even so, she was glad she had decided to make them this last time, even in his absence. As she scattered the cinnamon and raisins on the rolled out dough, she loved the fluff, the depth, and the puffiness already growing. Surrounded by the oven's warmth, the dough would rise and rise and make light, perfect rolls that she would bake, glaze and wrap in heated napkins as she had so many times before.

While they were in the oven, maybe she would page him and ask him to come home. He would think she meant for yet another baby-making tryst. He would leave his job reluctantly and head home because he was good like that. But this time, he would find her different, coy and outrageous, not to mention half-naked, and ready to love him for qualities not related to procreation.

She'd find something else to create, she was sure. Tears added salt to the dough, blended with the flour and fell on the robe, as she reached to the floor to pick it up. She used the robe to dab the egg from her stomach, using it to make her feel a little less naked while she dialed his number.

Peanut Butter

Their perfectly coordinated swimwear pleased her. Harmony existed between her dark green suit dotted with deep blue splotches, a little deep purple, almost black here and there, and her husband's blue-green cargo-style trunks. Their tiny son's swimsuit contained the best of them both, her deep blue, solid this time with her husband's blue-green in dots randomly splayed across Brandon's two-year-old derriere.

This harmony did not happen by accident. It had required many decisions, forays on lunch hours and after work into stores both cheap and expensive. Finally, and this was key, after spending hours trying on bathing suits, she found the one that complemented her long torso, adequate breasts and long lean legs, not to mention her deep green eyes and dark silky hair. If Brandon weren't attached to her at the hip, she was sure no one would ever think she had had a baby.

And now at last they were at the shore, all preparations having been completed, the arguing over who would do what to get ready behind them.

As Juliane carried the toddler over the boardwalk toward the ocean beach, she saw that the "No Trespassing" signs still were there, protecting the huge sand dunes from the damaging erosion that results from human feet trekking across the sand. These warnings were at least twenty-five years old, and had been there as long as her family had been visiting the Jersey shore.

Matt hadn't wanted to make this their vacation destination this summer. Atlantic City and the excitement of the casinos were more appealing to him, but Juliane had held out, remembering her childhood good times here, thinking of Brandon's enjoyment, thinking also that maybe she and Matt could reconnect after a busy year of toddler needs and Matt's needs and her needs all colliding at times.

"Next year, definitely the casinos, then. Somewhere where there is more action," Matt had said, sitting on the bed watching her pack. "It will be my turn to choose." He smiled, thinking of the action he dreamed that was there. "Hey, are these new?" He held up the green swim trunks she'd just folded and placed in his suitcase. "Not bad."

Juliane had just kept packing.

Matt arrived with the blanket, chairs and cooler, all coordinated in blues, greens and purples, and she sat Brandon in the sand while they staked out their corner of the beach. She tried to appear nonchalant as she smoothed out the blanket, feeling the eyes of the other beachgoers watching their progress, wondering if they were noticing the color coordination of her small family. But when she looked up, she realized they were looking past her, not at her.

She stood up and followed their gazes back toward the dune she had just crossed to see a group of men and boys dressed strangely for the beach, scampering down the boardwalk, exuberantly chasing the largest inner tube she had ever seen. It was the same height as the tallest of the men who were all dressed in dark blue jeans with elastic suspenders that crossed their backs. His shirt was gingham-checked, long sleeves rolled up and his straw hat was a tight weave with a thin black band. His eight or nine companions wore similar outfits.

The men had barely cleared the bluff when a group of women followed. Chatting and holding on to each other, there were twelve or thirteen in all, women and girls, wearing long dresses, mostly with puffed sleeves, all light cottons, pale pastels billowing in the wind. Some of the women, seemingly the older ones, wore tiny lace caps; others wore scarves holding their long hair back out of their faces. They tramped through the sand carrying small wicker baskets in the crooks of their arms, pointing and exclaiming at the height and force of the waves. They made attractive little noises of glee as they watched the men and boys make their way through the other bathers and sun worshippers, faster and faster, pushing the inner tube farther and farther ahead of them and finally into the water. The men all followed the tube, tossing shoes but not hats, into the sand to await their return. At the last minute, the hats were placed gently on a nearby blanket by the smallest boy.

In a minute, the men were wet, head to toe, splashing and smiling, pushing the tube from man to man and boy to boy. Their clothing was clinging to them, their faces full of freedom, big grins and wide smiles in their fair faces, their childlike fun bringing smiles to the faces of the onlookers.

"Mennonites," Matt said.

"Not Amish?" Juliane asked.

"No facial hair, for one thing. I read that Amish men don't shave after they marry. Also I don't think your basic Amish person would get so soaking wet. It's all about moderation. And I think they arrived in a bus. Amish wouldn't do that." Matt looked at her and smiled. "I rest my case."

43

"How do you know all this?"

"You pick up things in a law office. Not all our clients are citizens in the mainstream of society."

"Do Mennonites sue each other or outsiders?" she asked. "Doesn't seem right."

"I can't tell you. Confidential. " Matt said. He smiled and put his arms around her waist. "I'll take Brandon down to the water. And, don't worry. I'll stick to how we talked about getting him acclimated. Slowly."

Juliane watched her perfectly matched husband and son. Her husband strode confidently toward the water; to keep up, their son tiptoed quickly in the hot sand.

The sand, the water, the waves, the rocks, the shells and all the things she loved as a young girl discovering Neptune's playground for the first time were what she loved about the shore. She couldn't wait to see her son's reaction. She leaned back on her elbows, soaking up the salt air, the sun. Then a familiar scream jolted her body upright. She shaded her eyes with her hand against the brightness so she could see the shoreline. Her body was on full alert.

His body language—his tiny arms and legs rigid, eyes squinting, face fiery red—told her what she needed to know. Brandon hated the water. Her husband had let Brandon take the lead. But once his little feet touched the cold water and a wave splashed his knees, his lead was to make a beeline for the blanket and throw himself into Juliane's arms. She smoothed his hair back and tried to calm his crying, "No water. No water."

"Well, that didn't work," Matt said as he sat with them on the blanket. He always seemed surprised and put out at the unpredictability of a two-year-old. Brandon, now calm, sat on the blanket, grabbed his bucket and shovel and started digging. Matt looked around. His gaze moved toward a high-pitched shriek coming from the water.

"Wow," Matt said. "Those dresses are way more revealing than any bathing suit."

Juliane looked over. The Mennonite women and girls, previously standing in ankle-deep water, had been surprised by a rogue wave and were soaked to their waists. The light cotton of their dresses was clinging to their thighs and calves.

She stiffened and asked herself for the hundredth time why Matt always had to make comments about how other women looked. She always wondered if he did it to let her know he was looking at—and thinking about—other women.

Juliane paid attention to Brandon while her husband watched shapely young women in bathing suits wander the beach. She didn't like his constant commentary, though softly whispered, about the pros and cons, mostly pros, of the sweet young things on the beach. This must be what he considered action. A few looked his way and others smiled at him as they walked by. Maybe this action was at his office, too. Juliane shivered. She also didn't like the way she automatically compared herself to the girls he was looking at.

"Could you not be so obvious?" she said.

"Just think how disappointed they'd be if **they** spent hours picking out just the right suit that made them look good, and no one noticed," Matt said. He gave her what she privately referred to as his "guy" grin.

"An immature excuse for you to look at women who aren't your wife," she said.

She gazed over at the Mennonite women who were drying themselves with small, white towels. The tall man in suspenders stood, hands on hips, looking out over the sea as though there were something fascinating out there. In his wet jeans, rolled up to mid-calf, and shirt plastered to his torso, with his hair blowing in the breeze, she was jealous of how peaceful and in control he appeared.

"To be so happy with so little," she murmured.

"I'm hungry," Matt said. "What's for lunch?"

"Caesar chicken salads and baguettes. Fruit for dessert. And a cookie if you're good," she said.

"Who eats salad at the beach?" Matt said.

"We do," she said and smacked him in the chest with his salad container.

"No sandwiches?"

"Okay, sandwiches tomorrow," Juliane said. "Today it's salad. Time for lunch."

Juliane pulled Brandon to her and opened his salad container.

Brandon looked at her and at the food. Brandon didn't want any salad—fruit either.

"Noooo," he said. He took off running before she had a chance to grab him. She got up and pursued him but he was maintaining a pretty good lead. She found herself chasing him down the beach with the bowl of salad.

The smallest Mennonite boy intercepted him and crouched down to his level. Brandon was surprised and stopped. The boy started digging in the sand and Brandon crouched down with him.

"Hey, I'm digging a hole," the boy said, talking directly to Brandon, who was fascinated by the new person.

"We'll be okay here," the boy said to Juliane. "I saw he doesn't like the water much, but he will." He said this with a big smile.

"Okay," Juliane smiled back. "His name is Brandon. What's yours?"

"Jacob," he said.

Brandon, now fully engaged, was digging with his hands.

Juliane asked Jacob if he wanted to come closer to their blanket to play. He looked toward the man with hands on hips who had been watching the toddler drama. The man nodded to Juliane.

"Come back soon for lunch, Jacob," he called.

Juliane smiled her thanks. He nodded again.

Jacob was about eight but played well with a willful two-year-old. With the digging and the fort making, he was leading Brandon closer and closer to the water and now the water was seeping into their hole.

Jacob stood up and splashed in the puddle. Brandon did the same. The huge smile on his face made Juliane laugh. He waved at them. Juliane waved back and poked Matt to do the same.

Shortly, Juliane saw the man waving, trying to get Jacob's attention. She noticed the women were unpacking the baskets. Jacob started back for lunch and Brandon followed him. Juliane hopped up to pick Brandon up before he started to cry, but Jacob turned and asked if he could bring his lunch back and eat with them.

"If it's okay with your father, it's fine with me," she said.

"He's my Uncle Micah," Jacob said. "I'll ask him."

"I'll come with you."

When they neared the others, Jacob called out to the man. "May I take my lunch and eat with Brandon?"

The man nodded his head, reached into one of the baskets and pulled out a peanut butter and jelly sandwich on thick slices of homemade wheat bread. The peanut butter was thickly spread and overlapped the edges of the bread, smearing onto the man's hand.

Juliane put Brandon down and out of habit extended her hand. "I'm Brandon's mother."

He wiped his hand on his jeans. "I'm Jacob's Uncle Micah." His large hand was warm and completely covered hers. His handshake was firm.

"We'd love to have Jacob join us for lunch," she said. "The boys are playing so well together. You nephew is really good with him.

The man laughed. "He gets a lot of experience with the smaller children in our school."

"He's welcome to share our salads and desserts," she said.

"I'm sure his sandwich is fine, Ma'am," the man said, just as Jacob said, "Peanut butter is my favorite."

Just then, Brandon reached for Jacob's sandwich. "Sammich," he said.

"Here, son. You can have your own," the man said, chuckling. He reached into the basket for another sandwich and handed it to Brandon who immediately tried to bite through the plastic wrap. They all laughed. Juliane crouched down to remove half the sandwich and hand it to him. She was aware that the man was looking at her intently. Brandon took a big happy bite but held out his hand. He wanted to carry the half in the wrap as well.

"Lesson learned," she said ruefully. "Forget salads. At the beach, lunch is a sandwich and preferably peanut butter."

They looked at each other and smiled. His eyes were deep blue, and seemed to be silently laughing. At what? she thought. At my selection of inappropriate foods for the beach? My coming here to meet him personally? Or, oh God, is it my lack of a swimsuit cover up? She wished she had thrown on her coordinating terry cloth shift.

"Thank you for Brandon's sandwich," she said.

"Welcome, Ma'am."

She picked up her sandwich-munching son and walked toward their blanket with Jacob running ahead. Was the man watching her walk? What was he thinking?

At the blanket, Matt was finishing up his salad. She looked back toward the man.

"What are you looking at?" Matt asked.

"Jacob's uncle. He gave Brandon a peanut butter sandwich so he could eat with Jacob, although not as neatly, obviously." She rummaged through the beach bag for a wet wipe and cleaned the peanut butter smears from Brandon's mouth, cheeks and hair.

"Ahh," said Matt. "A manly lunch and a man's sandwich. Look at the size of that bread."

Juliane gave him a look.

"Nice of him to share with our little guy," Matt said. "Hey, when the kids are done eating, maybe a walk on the beach?"

"I'd rather stay on the blanket and bask," she said. "You guys just go."

The boys were enthusiastic about a walk. Jacob ran to ask his uncle who waved his permission to Juliane, and the three set off down the beach. Juliane watched as Jacob walked splashing just at the edge of the water. Brandon joined right in and didn't even mind when a large wave got his trunks wet. Matt looked back at her and pointed at Jacob with thumbs up.

She turned on her stomach on the blanket. It was hot and the sun's warmth soaked through her. She put her cheek on her hands and got a whiff of peanut butter. Impulsively, she licked her hand. It had a sweet, nutty taste. From Micah's hand, she thought. With her eyes closed and welcoming the relaxation that time without a two-year-old nearby can bring, she dozed off.

They are alone on the beach. The wind has picked up and her hair is blowing wildly in front of her face. The man pushes her hair back with a gentle caress. It's getting cooler, she says. The man removes his gingham shirt and places it over her shoulders. Come. He takes her hand. They walk the empty boardwalk and when they reach the no trespassing signs, he steps over the railing and reaches up to steady her as she follows. We shouldn't be here, she says. The sign. It's all right, he says. Come. They walk-slide down the dune. The man holds her close so she doesn't fall. The dune protects them now. There is no wind. She feels warm again. It's nice here, she says. She sits in the sand. He stands, hands on his hips. He looks at her with piercing blue eyes, saying nothing. She thinks he can see more than she wants him to. We're alone, she says. The way it should be, he says. The others? she asks. No others. Only you. He sits next to her, their shoulders touch. They look at each other. Their faces are close. She closes her eyes, awaiting and fearing the touch of his lips which she is sure will come. It's a slow start kiss, just at one side of her mouth. The kiss moves toward the center of her lips with the promise of more. His firm hand is on her shoulder turning her toward him and laying her back in the sand. So tender. She weeps.

"We're back." Matt was lightly shaking her shoulder.

Juliane sat up abruptly, so fast that she felt a little dizzy. Her face was wet.

"Mama, Mama!" Brandon shrieked, pointing to the large conch shell Jacob is holding.

"Had a nice walk," Matt said. "Brandon went in the water, thanks to Jacob." He ruffled Jacob's hair.

"I'm still hungry," Matt said. "Can I have the other half of that sandwich?" He rooted around in the cooler and took out the half sandwich. Brandon spied it and reached out his hand.

"Sammich," he said.

"Brandon, you can share with your father," said Jacob. The boy broke the half sandwich in half again. He handed Brandon his half with a big smile and the toddler happily plunked down in the sand.

Juliane looked over toward Jacob's group. Micah was vigilant, watching for his nephew. She wiped her face.

"You okay?" Matt said.

"Sand in my eye, I guess."

Matt took a bite. "This peanut butter even smells manly, he said. "Sometimes a peanut butter sandwich is just what you need." He winked.

"I'm beginning to see that, too," Juliane said softly, to the sea breeze.

Sugar Cubes

I've known since I was ten that life is not sugarcoated. I learned this when on a sunny mid-western afternoon, a man exposed himself to me and my sister; literally a big bad wolf as we truly were on our way to Grandma's house.

We had been at Don's, a corner grocery store, where we had turned our cache of hoarded coins into two brown bags of penny candy. It's not like either of us remembers the specifics other than we both stood there dumbfounded for a moment before we began to scream and run. We ran, following the cement walls of the creek bed, dry and full of weeds, holding tight to our candy bags until we couldn't make any more noise, so fast was our breathing. We weren't even near Grandma's yet. Looking behind us, we sprinted up the hill with our matching skirts and sweaters flapping in the wind we created. Then we tore down the alley filled with tiny rocks that pelted the knees and shins of whichever of us for the moment lagged behind, then finally up the worn carpet that covered the stairs to Grandma's apartment.

"Mommy," we both yelled, demanding her attention simultaneously as we so often did, even though at ten, I was three years older than my sister and was expected to be more mature. Our father was in the army, living in

Europe already, and we were staying with Grandma, waiting for the all clear to get on a plane and join him.

Our mother rushed out of the back room with pins in her mouth as she so often did when she was helping Grandma make someone's wedding gown or business suit. When she asked us what was the matter, we were still gasping for breath. We looked at each other, each hoping the other would have the right words, but we were both nearly speechless.

"A man," I croaked, "a man was at the creek." I saw my mother's look of alarm. "A man, and he opened a rain coat. And he showed us—that." My use of the nonspecific pronoun notwithstanding, our mother got the message and hurried to call the police, who found our situation threatening enough to promise a visit right away. As our mother talked to the authorities, my sister looked at me with her big blue eyes, as wide as I'd ever seen them, and I heard her whisper, "I want Daddy now." I hugged her but I knew he couldn't drop everything and head home.

I could sense our independence disappearing. No more trips to Don's. No more errands for Grandma resulting in tips to spend frivolously. Not that we would have wanted to go again, at least that day, for the thought of the man showing us that again was too frightening, even if we didn't know any of the words like pervert or pedophile, any of those terms that my mother would write to my father, stationed overseas, protecting the nation but unable to protect us from any of this.

"Girls, girls," my grandmother said, walking swiftly out of her sewing room, pushing the curtain that served as a door aside and swooping us toward the warmth and comfort of the kitchen. She steered us toward the kitchen table that fit into the corner like the last piece of a puzzle, cozy and tight. It was where our parents and aunts and uncles always sat as they dunked sugar cubes in their coffee, talking for hours about family and politics and the ways of the world.

She reached into the cupboard for four coffee cups and efficiently turned the gas on under the coffeepot on her way to the table. "We'll have these," she said in her Norwegian way with that lilt to her voice, plunking the yellow box of sugar cubes on the vinyl tablecloth so hard that they rattled. When the coffee was hot, we each got a cup, half full of hot coffee and half full of milk. And we each got sugar cubes for dunking.

I knew, from the few times I'd sneaked a sugar treat, that the great thing about sugar cubes was that you could stick just the corner into the coffee and watch the brown color seep into the granules. Then you could suck the coffee out of it, sweetened beyond belief, and the cube would begin to disintegrate almost before you could pop it in your mouth. I had observed that when adults ate them, they talked more and laughed more.

My mother and grandmother did not limit our consumption of the sugar cubes that day. We dunked them and sucked them and ate them just the way we had seen the grownups do. We talked and laughed too, and I knew then that the reason our aunts and uncles did it was because there were things about the world that were sour and the sugar cubes could make them sweet. I felt that being part of this was a privilege, a reward, and a cure.

I don't remember exactly what the four of us talked about but I do know that my mother's and grandmother's attention was all for us, no more care for the bride or the business woman who would be without gown or suit if they needed them any time soon. We sat in the corner around that table, our circle protecting us—the husband—

the father— not with us, serving some higher calling so far away, the sugar cubes as close as the nearest cupboard.

Peeling Potatoes

I t was in the kitchen of their apartment in Odense, Denmark, the birthplace of Hans Christian Andersen, that Janie's mother decided to talk to her, for the first time, about sex. At age twelve, Janie was no stranger to moving and living in foreign places. However, in the turmoil of adjusting and readjusting to schools and friends and countries, one constant her parents insisted on, as much as possible, was a routine family life. So, no matter where the U.S. Government sent their family to live, helping to prepare dinner was one of her assigned chores. She was dutiful about it and good at it, and, on this particular afternoon, the galley kitchen in the apartment made her a captive audience.

Janie just had dumped a bag of potatoes into the sink and covered them with water. Some were still coated with dirt that started to loosen; some of the dirt sank and some of it rose to the top. She was on the verge of asking her mother the scientific basis for the sinking or floating of dirt, because more than half the fun of helping her mother make dinner was spending time with her. They would chat about how Janie was doing at her Danish school and whether she was happy with her new friends, or they might just talk about fun nonsense. On this day though, her mother was no nonsense, as she stood at the stove between

Janie and the kitchen door, concentrating on browning a huge piece of beef.

Smoke from the beef had filled the kitchen, creeping toward the open window, making her mother look like a vision, tall and thin, in an apron that protected the delicately rendered posies on her cotton shirtwaist dress, the style of the late 1950s. The fragrance of the well-seasoned meat being seared in onion was tantalizing and evoked thoughts of what would accompany it—her mother's cloud-like mountain of mashed potatoes and the thick, dark gravy she would magically create out of seemingly nothing important, just several tablespoons of meat drippings and flour and the water from the potatoes Janie herself was preparing.

She reached in front of her mother for the potato peeler, wondering if this time she actually would get to cut the potatoes, create four pieces out of one whole. Usually Janie only got to do the peeling, then piled the near-ready potatoes next to the stove for her mother to quarter, a task that she deemed as yet too dangerous for her daughter.

This time, though, her mother didn't stop Janie as she reached for the knife and set it next to the growing pile of potatoes she was creating; instead her mother smiled and moved out of her way. She smelled like perfume and braised beef. Her face glowed with the new make-up she had applied, her hair shone with the brushing she had given it, all to welcome her husband, Janie's father, home from the government office where he worked all day.

Her mother began with a question. "Honey, I'm just curious." She turned to face Janie. "Do you know how babies are made?"

Janie sucked in air and held her breath. She didn't answer, gaze fixed on the eyes of the potato she clutched even harder and peeled with even greater concentration. It was a very large potato with thick brown skin flaked with little plugs of dirt, a potato bought at the pig farm just one-half mile from their suburban housing development outside of Odense. Janie was grateful for its size because it would take her a while to peel and she wouldn't have to look up at her mother for at least that long. Her mother looked over at her, her look continuing her question, and Janie shook her head.

They didn't make eye contact as they stood side by side; the mother searing, the daughter peeling, mother talking, daughter listening, nearly shoulder to shoulder in the narrow space.

Janie did have a vague idea about the origin of babies and certainly had wondered about it. She had seen the huge stork's nest on the thatched roof of the pig farmer's house and at the Hans Christian Andersen House and Museum, too, and her father had joked with Janie and her younger sister about the stork and her baby brother, and he had winked at her, the oldest, as though she knew better. She remembered that day and considered that maybe her lack of response to that wink had made her parents look in that Dr. Spock's child-rearing book on the bookshelf in the living room to find out what a pre-teen girl should know—and when.

"When two people really love each other, they want to be close to each other," her mother said, clearing her throat and concentrating on the searing. "Sometimes that means taking their clothes off so they can be even closer and then they…"

She kept talking and turning the meat. Soon the air was acrid with a burning smell and the crusty exterior of the round roast was covered with the burned onions stuck to it.

"You're burning the meat," Janie wanted to scream, "and I can't breathe." But she would have had to interrupt and as embarrassing as it was listening, it was fascinating, too. So, Janie continued peeling until her mother stopped talking and asked, "Okay?"

Janie nodded her head and looked at her mother quickly because she knew her mother would require knowing that she had understood, and that she was okay.

"Questions? Ask me anything," her mother said but Janie shook her head.

Satisfied, her mother removed the meat from the frying pan and put it in the Dutch oven, then opened the oven door and slid the pot inside. She chatted about this and that, adding meaningless conversation to the important monologue they just had shared. Janie cut the last potato into quarters, then, on an impulse, into eighths. Her mother watched her cut those pieces, make them a little too small, but she didn't comment as she would have in the past, usually trying to nudge Janie, however gently, one step closer to her personal pursuit of perfection and order.

Janie's head ached from the overload of new information and from all the questions that were churning in her brain, questions she was too embarrassed to ask. She wiped her hands on the dishtowel and turned to the door. Looking over her shoulder, she told her mother that she was going out to play before dinner. She felt, more than saw, her mother nod that that would be okay.

Even years later, opening a bag of potatoes, or creating the cloud-like mound for her own family, Janie sometimes could smell the dirt, feel the rhythmic scrape of the peeler, relish the moist starch against her palms, could savor the crisp sound of the potato being reduced into quarters, then eighths. But from that day, what she mostly remembered is that when she went outside to play, there was air out there. It smelled clean and crisp. She had breathed deeply, and sucked the air into her lungs, her blood pumping from a more mature heart, one that could be broken, mended, affected by the whims of boys, and in the future, men.

Dark Chocolate

F reedom. Freedom. Freedom. There. I said it out loud three times like I did at the beginning of every summer. The delicious "f" sound shot forth from my lips, then the "dom," to be distinguished from dumb, because school was out and smart or dumb was a thing of the past, at least for the next few months. This ritual repetition was essential to the start of my summer. I couldn't give it up; it was so integral to my summer enjoyment, my joy.

I looked forward to the euphoria of sun-drenched days, my back warm on the pavement of our driveway where I liked to recline, looking up at the rolling heavens. One minute there would be sun, the next minute clouds, fluffy white against bright blue. Sometimes I would come prepared with a milk chocolate bar and nibble it while I wondered what was up there, how crowded it was, what with God, the angels, Thor and his gang, relatives, friends, and everyone else who had aspired to and achieved a spot.

Or, armed with a dark chocolate bar, I might ponder what went on below, where the heat on my back could be coming from, the down-under, Lucifer, Hades, the River Styx, and all that we thought was down there, where my best friend said all the interesting people would be anyway.

All wondering and pondering aside, the bottom line was that I had to have a summer job, and since getting a really good job required me to be older, a baby-sitting position for two toddlers of French teachers was my plight. It would take my whole day, eight to four, Monday through Friday, but I could stand it, because I knew though I might be there in body, in mind and spirit I'd be gone to my secret place. My mind would wander, lining up what I someday would write, my novel, my magazine articles, my stories, the words I would put together that people would queue up to buy and to read. My spirit would be free from studying, from chores, from being liked or hated by schoolmates, from the pressure of being nice all the time.

This was the summer I would discover what I wanted to be, how I wanted to behave, what I wanted from life. After all, miracles had happened over the past year. My acne had cleared up, my braces were off, my chest was developing nicely, my chestnut brown hair finally was the length I liked it—all in all, when I looked in the mirror, I now considered myself someone to be desired. I was anticipating the possibilities. I was sixteen.

And as it happened, on the first day of my baby-sitting job, I discovered that all I wanted from life was the undivided attention of a boy named Ray.

I had walked with the two cherubs, one in a stroller, the other tugging at my shorts, down to the corner drugstore to look at the latest teen magazine. I had been to the drugstore a million times, and for nine hundred ninety-nine thousand, nine hundred and ninety-nine, the trip had been ho-hum. On this day, there was Ray. I knew of him and had seen him around now and then. He would be a senior next fall and hung with a much faster crowd than my mother would approve of. As their cars roared down the busy street toward the cemetery just as the sun was setting, high-pitched girl laughs and deep-throated boy laughs flowed out the windows and trailed after the cars as they cruised through the iron gates. I was sure they drank.

He was waiting on my friend Donna at the soda counter and she actually was flirting with him. I'd never seen Donna do that, always thought she was too self-conscious to approach anyone of Ray's caliber, and he was high caliber. I pushed and dragged the kids up to where she sat drooling into her cherry coke, and she said hello to me as if I was an afterthought. Ray was further down the counter and as I watched him prepare a hot fudge sundae with extra fudge, I knew that I had to find a way to get his attention. This would not be easy, since any bravado I had was directly from the fantasy world I had created for my shy self. But, my desperation to achieve my personal goal, whatever it might be for this sixteenth summer, made me bold and I looked him directly in the eye and ordered a chocolate coke. This was a very new thing in 1963, in our area of suburban Boston. Many people who had tried it said it required a sophisticated palate. Ray asked if I had the stomach for it and I said yes, anyone who could watch *Psycho* without flinching during the shower scene could easily handle a chocolate coke. I could see his respect for me deepen when he heard that, and he volunteered that *Psycho* was his favorite movie. I lied and said it was mine, too, and did he want to go to the drive-in to see it with me again on Saturday. My heart, which had been just pounding away, nearly stopped beating as I waited for his reply.

At that point the baby started wailing for no reason and nothing I could do, no shaking of the rattle or poking of the bottle into her mouth, could calm her. I was getting rather frantic myself as everyone, including Ray, was staring at me and at her.

65

"Let me," he said and lifted her out of the stroller. She stopped crying immediately. He walked her around the store, pointing out this and that, and talking to her in a calm and playful voice. By the time he handed her to me, I had decided he was to be the father of my children. As he walked back around the counter, he said, "Saturday. Seven-thirty."

Five cars were parked in our row on the raised bump of asphalt that pointed them toward the movie screen. The sound of fresh popcorn popping and the delicious fragrance filled the area closest to the snack bar, which is where Ray had gone. I wished fleetingly that we had parked closer to it where there was more light. He approached the car with candy bars sticking out of his pockets and more popcorn and soda than a human could possibly carry—but then he wasn't human.

He was a god, idolized by all my girlfriends, for his deep brown eyes, and curly thick hair, his taut lean physique, the jeans he always wore just so. His husky voice and quick wit were offered with an underlying sensuality that caused all my friends to infuse their conversations with approach and then avoidance strategies, one minute arguing for going out with him, the next explaining why they couldn't.

"Got it," he said, somehow opening the car door himself and sliding in without spilling a kernel.

Yes, you do, I thought.

The Superman beach towel that protected the leather seats of his immaculate classic Buick got a little messed up but he quickly straightened it and settled in for the movie.

I thought it was cute that he was particular about his car. I had seen him lovingly stroke its chrome mirror as he waited for me in front of the house, and watched him wipe a speck of dust from the dashboard when we stopped for a red light.

The first show of the double feature began but I wasn't sure what it was or who was in it. All I was sure of was that I wanted to, was going to, do something—something I could tell my friends and dream of for months; how he used his hands, how his kiss stirred my most profound center, how creatively he seduced me, bringing me to the point where I didn't want to say no, yet I did, so sweetly and innocently that his heart melted. In my fantasy, he was so affected by my sweetness, that, in fact, he was smitten—God I loved that word—just smitten, and he couldn't think of anything or anyone else, just me. Of course, the feeling would be mutual and we'd save the ultimate togetherness for our wedding night. We'd agree on that, so changed would he be by my tender love.

"Want some candy bar?" he asked, bits of popcorn stuck between his front teeth. He was intent on the screen.

"No thanks." I slowly sipped my ultra large cola, hoping I wouldn't have to go to the ladies room before all these life-changing events happened, or worse yet, during.

On screen, a god-like hero was beginning the make-out ritual with the female lead. His hand was on her neck, his thumb stroking her throat, his lips barely touching hers. I just knew his tongue would be next, then he would press against her, she would back into the wall and fall uncontrollably, helplessly, under his sensuous spell.

In the darkness, I glanced sideways at my male lead, hoping for the smoldering look I knew he was capable of, that he was saving for just the right moment. He felt my glance and turned to me.

"Last bite," he offered. He extended a candy bar in my direction.

"Merci," I was inspired to say, in my best French.

The huskiness and foreign sound in my voice must have surprised him. As he moved closer to hand me my piece of the chocolate, I leaned forward with my eyes closed, and shook my long dark hair down over one eye. Then I waited, lips parted, tongue extended for the taste, imagining myself to look like every movie heroine I'd ever watched. The scoop neck on my summer dress scooped out and I knew he could see my new white lacy bra.

He fed me the confection and did not turn his attention back to the screen. He reached for me, hand on the back of my neck, pulling me toward him, I was sure, for a gentle touching of lips, a sharing of the sublime taste of chocolate, the last of the candy, sweetness in the dark.

Gentle nothing, I remember thinking as his chocolate lips attacked mine. I gasped as he pushed himself on top of me, as his hands roughly groped the shoulder straps off my shoulder and settled themselves on the lacy cups of my bra. No finesse, I remember thinking as he groped under my skirt, his hands as insistent as mine were defensive. For a moment I wanted to make it all stop, but I would have embarrassed myself by screaming, and that would only bring the security guard to the car window, and he knew my parents. But I was sixteen and this was my summer and this was my adventure, not Ray's, so I moaned loudly and kissed him the way it said to in the sex manual my friends and I had bought in an antique bookstore in Harvard Square—and devoured. The book said it was a kiss guaranteed to control a man. The kiss was long and when I was through, I ran my fingers through his hair. Miraculously he stopped groping and looked at me with something like the same respect as he had when I ordered the chocolate coke. Our kisses after that were tender, his hand on my neck, a lighter touch, his hands on my breasts gentle and the rest of what we did was what I would allow and it was enough for me, for that night.

And for several weeks after, every Saturday we had the same drive-in date, different movies but the same plot, for us to be together, to touch each other, to share candy bars in a way that their creators would never dare advertise.

I'm sure my friends were jealous and surprised by the turn of events. The goodiest of two shoes gets the handsome prince. My friends should have remembered that princes were attracted to innocence and their wildness was tamed by it. And the princes never seemed to resent it, so enchanted were they.

But my prince was getting restless. He became moody and cranky and instead of accepting my limits, he would push and cajole. The evenings that used to end with delicate kisses and soft caresses began to end with a rougher edge. It was exciting in a way I wasn't eager to admit to anyone, so I didn't. As it all got more serious, he seemed less like a boy and more like a man. In so many ways he pushed me to go all the way and as for me, I allowed more and more, afraid to lose the best thing I had, the thing that all others coveted and had no idea what hard work it was to keep it.

The worst thing was, I was not happy. The thrill of seeing him pull up in front of the house and seeing the neighbors stop their yard work or pause in the dog walking to look, was turning into dread. Evenings would start out innocently enough. We'd get a burger, fool around with his friends and then cruise to the cemetery to drink beer, which I never really did as drinking was against my personal code. All the guys, especially Billy Cameron, tried to get me to have some, as if it were their job to make me let down my guard. Probably they would have lost interest if it weren't for Ray captivated by, as I've said before, my sweetness, my promise, and the fact that my chest chose these months to expand even more and that was an area I would let him freely explore. It seemed I was a natural at moaning, moaning incredibly and realistically, and for a while that was enough, but I had heard from other girls that guys wanted more, always more. I knew I was reaching an impasse where I would have to put out or shut up, and the more I knew Ray, the more I doubted he should be the first. I knew he talked about other girls he'd been with, although not to me, and I didn't want to be just another of his stories, to be talked about so lewdly and compared with so many. One other thing I knew for sure was that this summer was not through being my adventure; I just wasn't quite sure how I wanted it to play out.

It was at this point that I began to rely heavily on candy bars.

Ray had a definite weakness for them, especially dark chocolate ones. I had observed how he used them in his life, to stay awake, to get energy, to get aroused as he smeared chocolate on me, then licked it off. So I kept three candy bars with me always and pulled them out as needed and so far they had worked as distractions in those pivotal moments, allowing me some leeway, some protection while still keeping Ray interested. At least I thought so.

However, I was becoming increasingly embarrassed by the chocolate stains in different and interesting locations on my clothes. My mother had to be suspicious when I started doing my own laundry. I would soak clothes in tubs full of cold water under my bed so she wouldn't ask any questions I would have to ignore. I even surprised myself with what I, former goody two shoes, was willing to do, the lengths to which I would consider compromising my basic self, to hang on to Ray.

Then one Friday night Billy Cameron tried once more to lure me into having a beer at the cemetery. I had been sitting there quietly on the mausoleum steps, incredulous still at being one of the girl voices laughing as the cars cruised through town. Billy took a swig from his quart bottle, wiped the top with his shirtsleeve and handed me the bottle.

I shook my head and Billy laughed. "What's so funny?" I whispered. I always whispered in the cemetery.

He sat down too close to me and he laughed louder. "I don't believe it," he said. "You're so stupid."

"What?" I whispered louder, trying to scoot away.

"Where do you think he is now?" Billy asked, his face too close to mine.

"Getting more beer and chocolate bars," I offered self-righteously, since that's where Ray had told me he was going. "When he gets back we're going to the drive-in," I added.

"Yeah, if you say so," Billy said. His face was one big smirk.

"Where do you think he is?" I asked the question louder than I should have.

"Shhh." Billy cupped his hand across my mouth.

"Okay, okay," I whispered again, pushing his hand away. "Stop it. Where is he then, big shot?"

"In the car. Over by the reflecting pond." Billy said innocently. "With Alicia."

Having dropped that bomb, he finished the beer and waited. He didn't have to wait long as I got right up and started toward the pond, my heart pounding and my temper rising. Billy tried to hold me back. He pulled on my arm, and grabbed my sweater which I tried to twist out of so I could keep going. After I got free from the sweater and, I thought, from Billy, I started to run to get away from

71

him. I was fast but he was right behind me. The car was there all right, and it was bouncing and creaking. "See," he said, breathing heavily. "You can't keep being a tease."

I had never thought of myself as a tease. To me, I was just working my summer adventure, completing my plan. When Billy threw that word my way, I stopped short. He ran into me, knocking me down in the leaves. Before I knew it, he was on me, holding my hands over my head and trying to kiss me with his beery mouth. I tried to scream but he covered my mouth with his and with one of his hands, tried to unzip my shorts. I bit his lip hard, causing him to curse, and rolled out from under him, screaming Ray's name. The car was still bouncing and creaking. I clawed my way through the clippings from the newly cut grass toward the car, still screaming Ray's name but Billy was on me again, rolling me over and this time not bothering with my hands but going straight for zippers, both mine and his.

This is not my adventure, this is not my adventure, I kept saying to myself as I pummeled him in the face and on the back with one hand, the other holding my shorts tightly to me.

"Stop it, stop it," I screamed. "Ray," I shrieked. My shorts ripped and I started to cry. The car just kept on bouncing and creaking.

Suddenly there was a scream from the car, one like I had never heard before. It was a girl's scream, one that started low and reached a higher pitch each time the car rocked. It wasn't a scream of fright or pain, more like a sound of desperation and delight if that makes sense, getting more desperate as the car rocked more violently. The sound stopped Billy for a moment and I took the opportunity to heave him off me and run for the car.

Now we were both calling Ray's name, me for salvation, Billy for warning. As I reached the car, I heard Ray cry out, too. I snatched open the back door, and was immediately sorry, seeing them there, entangled in their half-removed clothing, but connected at one very obvious point. Their faces were a freeze-frame of total disbelief, Alicia irritated as she usually was in my presence, Ray looking at my face, seeing the tears, the grass in my hair, the state of my clothes.

No one said anything now. Ray, like the gentlemen he was not, extricated himself from Alicia, not caring about her level of disarray, then nonchalantly reached for and pulled up his jeans as though he did this all the time. Tears were blurring my vision but still I saw Alicia skulk out the other car door and disappear into the shrubbery that surrounded the pond.

"What's up?" Ray said, looking at Billy who could not look him in the eye, and then at me who could barely look at him at all. "What happened?" He tried again at which point I started crying hysterically, gasping for breath, terrified at what had almost happened to me and incensed at what had happened in the car.

"Billy jumped me," I sobbed. "First he told me to come here and find you and then he followed me and tried to rape me. Rape me! And he's your friend and he tried to rape me." The word rape felt jagged and cutting in my mouth. "What are you going to do about it?" I yelled, punching him in the torso for many reasons.

"Hey. Hey," he said, grabbing my hands. He waited a few seconds and then said, "He's drunk. Nothing happened, did it? Nothing real, did it? You're okay, aren't you? He's just drunk."

"I want to go home," I yelled, stepping up close, my face in Ray's face. "Take me home."

He held the car door for me, first time ever, and drove me directly to the drive-in.

"I want to go home," I repeated, sniffling, when I realized where we were going.

"Relax," Ray said in his soft, baby-calming voice. "We'll just watch the movie and calm down a little. Then I'll take you home."

I looked at the lips that had kissed Alicia, at the arms that had held her, at the hands that had undone her clothing and touched her in some of the places they had touched me. I did not want those parts of Ray to touch me ever again.

"I'll get you some popcorn," he said, as though nothing were different. I said nothing as he left the car but I knew I wouldn't touch anything he brought me. As I turned to watch him go, the car creaked, the same creaking as by the reflecting pond, and I knew I couldn't stand to be in that car for another minute. When I grabbed my purse, my three emergency candy bars fell onto the seat. My first thought was to just leave them, a last remembrance of what we had, something that would make Ray sorry for what he had done to me, to my trust, to my adventure.

My second, more pressing, thought was to get even. I looked out to make sure he was in a long popcorn line. He was. I grabbed the candy bars and held them in my hot palms until they started to feel even more squishy than they were from being in my purse. I unwrapped them, then rubbed the chocolate all over everything I could in the car: the steering wheel, gearshift, radio knobs, the door handle, the window lock, the pristine leather seats that Ray had so carefully covered with his stupid Superman beach towel. All these things became brown and sticky in short order and I hoped it was warm enough to keep them that way. I got out of the car, carefully smearing his door handle with chocolate as well. I quickly used the last bit of chocolate to scribble on the front windshield and then I made for the back rows where I hoped Donna and several of my girl friends would be, actually watching the movie.

I started out walking as fast as I could, but when the opening credits began to scroll down the screen, I began to run. When I saw Donna's car a few rows back, I sprinted for it, licking the bittersweet chocolate from my fingers, not looking back.

The Casserole

Hot sausage could spice up almost anything, her mother often had said as Carole was growing up. And Carole remembered this most clearly the first time that Gary had come for dinner. But after he helped her clear the table, and put away the dishes, and then get comfortable on the daybed in her apartment, she recalled that by then, the heat had nothing to do with the food.

That casserole she had thrown together on their first date was made from the things her mother said good cooks always have handy. Hot sausage, onions, tomatoes, green peppers, garlic, spices, cheese, and pasta—all ingredients that separately did not excite, but together produced tastes and textures that could satisfy even the most particular palate.

And Gary's palate had been particular, oh yes. Carole hadn't known his expectations for the culinary skills of a life mate on that first dinner date, but she could tell her casserole had passed muster. She knew by his small sounds of pleasure as he took the first bites, delving into the cheesy topping with a vengeance, savoring the sweetness of the onions chopped large, and the piquant taste of the peppers, blanched beforehand—he even commented on it—to make them soft and flavorful.

The sausage, where had she gotten it, he had asked, holding a piece on his fork, looking at it tenderly, commenting enthusiastically on its unique flavor. She had taken extra pains to go to the Italian market down the street for the sausage and had chosen hot, not mild—why mild, when hot sausage could spice up almost anything, when heat was what she felt from Gary, even sitting a desk away in ethics class, or next to him in a Vietnam history seminar in college.

So culinary magic had been one of the staples of their marriage, which had resulted in three children, a Victorian house in the cultural district, and a job for her as a cooking instructor for the local museum classes, and for him as an electrical engineer.

They lived a good life, had the good marriage, and did much of the cooking together. In the early years, they enjoyed chatting while mincing garlic cloves, sitting quietly together foraging through cookbooks for new challenges, and on weekends especially, for a long time, indulging in leisurely dinner preparations in which wine selections, dessert choices, candlelight and music were de rigueur.

Gary would stop at the little bakery on the west side of town to get her favorite ciabetta bread and she would always look for the perfect wine, Chianti, his favorite. He liked hot spices in his food and she did too, but only sometimes, so she would make her portion tolerable, and the rest to his liking. He liked her flexibility and adventurousness with spices; she, his attention to detail in procuring just the exactly right ingredients. These characteristics left little to chance and there were rarely fiascos in the kitchen.

When their three children were infants and toddlers, it was only after bedtime that Carole and Gary prepared and ate their dinner and had their time alone.

The high chair trays of all three stuck in her memory for their distinctive remains; Robbie, the oldest left anything green; Kate, the middle one, anything spicy; Timmy, even then, left anything that contained meat.

When the children were in nursery school, Carole and Gary's time alone further was reduced and every Friday, they put the children to bed a little earlier than normal and tried to enjoy cooking and each other as they once had, and sometimes they could.

But as the children got older, Carole lobbied for including them in the Friday ritual, which initially the children thought geeky but gradually came to enjoy as a time to relax, not in front of TV or under the basketball hoop, but with each other.

It was not surprising that the casserole was the family favorite, and that no matter what ingredients she used, hot sausage was a staple. The familiar was always welcome, so there was Carole making the casserole, sometimes for comfort on a cold and rainy day, and Carole making the casserole and freezing it for an emergency dinner. And there was Carole creating variations around the sausage that were sometimes welcome, sometimes not and on those times the chorus of "Mom, this isn't **the** casserole," or "Carole, can't you ever just use the recipe we know and love?" That last comment, always Gary's, had started to rankle—the "know" and "love" taking Carole, for a moment, back to that time, the daybed, the early years of perfection, now imperfectly remembered.

Carole and Gary's pride in their children grew as they did, but Carole missed her time alone with Gary. However, if he missed her, too, he didn't say, and eventually they, who had shared everything, barely spoke, even about the important things. It was at this time when she realized she was talking to everyone but Gary about what involved him the most.

Carole wasn't sure whether it had been Gary or the kids from whom she had needed relief, a change from the dreaded norm, when she had spent that month at the lake, that glorious time away. But she deserved that summer. She thought of it fiercely, defensively, even years later.

"I just need some time to myself," she had said.

"Let's all go," Gary had replied.

"You can't take a month off, and I want, I need to be gone, to be by myself for a while," she said, using the broken record technique she had read about in a women's magazine, saying the same thing in many ways.

"Then at least take Kate."

"I need some time away from kid stuff."

"What if I need time away?"

"I just need to get away for a while."

Finally he gave in, grudgingly, and with a mix of exhilaration and resentment, she drove north, away from the everyday things that encroached on their lives, remembering Gary's honest and caring face, troubled, and she remembered, after she returned, the unasked question between them.

It had been a cool New Hampshire early summer at Aunt Helen's cottage. The lake seemed to be just waking up, and the early morning mist was reminiscent of eerie fairy tale swamps where magical creatures hid.

The first day was restful, and Carole thought, just what she needed. But, on the second day, Joni Mitchell on compact disc being nowhere near enough company, it was apparent that a daily walk to the nearby small town of

Antwerp was going to be a must. Carole sauntered down to the general store, which was complete with a porch and a barrel and a few chairs where the locals sat chewing over the day's happenings.

Something for dinner, she was thinking as she pushed open the heavy carved door, very unlike the automatic doors in the large supermarkets she frequented. The lighting consisted of quaint, mismatched lamps and several unexpected skylights. This gave a cozy feel to the several small rooms, packed with, it seemed, more specialty than day-to-day grocery items, offering perhaps a bit of sophistication for the lake dwellers.

"New blood. Welcome."

Carole turned and behind a counter filled with jars of penny candies, saw a good-looking man smiling at her. He looked a little familiar.

"You're thinking Richard Gere, right?" the man said.

"Now that you mention it ..." Carole said. She could see it, the wavy hair, deep eyes and chiseled features. He had the lean look as well.

The man grinned. "The regulars are used to me so you are definitely new here."

Carole laughed out loud. "The Crawford place," she said.

"Nice lake view."

"The best."

He extended his hand. "Lou Ciardi."

"Carole Crawford," she said, shaking his hand. "And, how do you become a regular?"

"I guess I'd have to know all about you and have heard other people gossip about you. That seems to be the Antwerp way."

"I see." She smiled. "How much about me do you have to know?"

"Well, let's see. For you to be a regular, I need to know where you are from, what you are doing here, how long you will stay, what your eating habits are, what movies you like, what you read. Oh, and if you are married. That last one is just my own curiosity."

Flirting. A lost art buried in the lake regions of New England. Good-looking. And a younger man. A woman always knows. Fifteen years younger at least.

Another customer walked in and Carole wandered through the store, picking up interesting cans and boxes and bags and began selecting items to make an evening meal. But she was having trouble concentrating.

Then, in addition to an exotic rice pilaf mix, she picked up the ingredients for the casserole. Funny, she thought, even here at the lake with no one near, no one to cook for, that I am searching for those ingredients.

"Looks like a casserole in the making," Lou said, peering over her shoulder into her basket.

"You're sure?"

"Oh yeah. Anything with pasta and tomatoes, sausage and onions, any member of the Ciardi family would throw into a casserole on a cool night. Of course the accompaniments would be lots of wine and ciabetta.

"Sounds like a great family time."

"For sure. Or a romantic evening."

"I have a dish I make, a casserole really, not Italian, but nevertheless a family hand-me-down recipe. Also good for cool nights or rainy days. And it always starts with hot sausage. Actually, lately I've been thinking I might like to vary it a little, try something different, you know."

"Like?"

"Like if you had turkey sausage, I might buy that instead. Three color pasta, I'd use that. My own canned tomatoes in spices, I'd still throw that in. Maybe even

82

some portobellos. And since I'm not using hot sausage, I could add my own heat, a little cayenne or hot sauce maybe.

"Well, surprise. I have those things, all except for your homemade canned tomatoes, but I have something you could substitute." He came from behind the counter and reached for a glass jar with a familiar gourmet label. "That sounds like an indulge yourself recipe."

"Whenever I feel like it."

"Sounds great," Lou said. "Feel like company?"

"I guess." She said this slowly and thought of a hundred reasons why her answer should have been different.

"When?"

"Aren't you a little pushy?"

"Hey, you don't look like Richard Gere for nothing," he said. And then he smiled the crooked grin that had won the heart of Julia Roberts, Debra Winger and so many actresses she couldn't remember them all, and often Carole's heart as well.

As Carole took the glass jar from his hand, she felt a certain heat. She removed the customary ingredients from her basket and, with Lou's help, found the turkey sausage, three color pasta, some spices and a few other things. She said day after tomorrow would be fine.

She walked slowly back to the cottage, weighed down by the heavy packages and surprised by her behavior. But she was allowed to have men friends. One of her women friends at coffee before she left should have reminded her that it was dangerous to look at younger men as anything other than someone to help carry the grocery bags out to the car.

Back at the cottage, the shining beauty of the water beyond the long dock was exciting. She reveled in the calm of sitting at dock's end, with a glass of the coldest white wine, her gauzy dress moving with the soft breeze. She had bought several long and lightweight dresses and shirts for this time away, not her usual style, which was more tailored and crisp, and as her dress billowed with the currents of the breeze, she felt it was not only the dresses that were different here.

The night he came for dinner, the unexpected coolness and the dampness at the cottage called out for the comfort of a hot meal. She'd put the casserole together in just a few minutes. Lou, leaning on the doorjamb with a glass of wine glimmering in the sunset, watched her, chatting about his job, feelings about the lake, a give and take that she enjoyed so much more for the everyday lack of it. She liked the way Lou looked at her and talked to her, not through her, not as though he had said everything a million times before. And yet, it was odd being the performer, the sole preparer of the casserole.

"Feels a little strange," she said.

"How so?"

"The ingredients aren't the same."

"That could be exciting," he said.

"It's an odd mix."

"Let's see how it turns out."

During the past week, she had talked more to Lou in her daily visits to the store than she would sometimes say to Gary all day. And she became aware that in the speaking and the talking, desire becomes something you can touch, and finally you do touch it, holding the hand of a Richard Gere look-alike as you sit together on the dock with a second bottle of wine, well-fed and beguiled by a full moon. A spark connects you and it generates a kiss and the electricity increases until the voltage is way too high and must have an outlet which it seeks in the chintz-upholstered glider on Aunt Helen's porch.

The glider rocked like a pendulum, back and forth, Carole reaching for him like a much-missed lover. She was sure his eyes were asking and the more they asked, the more certain her answer.

Later, they lay together looking out at the lake, shimmering white, lit by the moon. Even with his arms around her, Carole felt cold.

"Thank God, it's dark," Carole murmured, stirring, buttoning her shirt and arranging her long skirt.

Lou felt around on the floor for his shirt.

"That was delicious," he said quietly. "The food and the dessert."

"I've never used quite that combination of spices before,"

"Something new for your cooking class."

"Something new for me," Carole said and Lou squeezed her hand.

"Let's go in," he said.

The chemistry was both exciting and comfortable and conversation with Lou was sweet, and like the green peppers in the casserole it added a sweet taste to her life, a sweetness that even tinged with guilt, she liked.

Over the next few weeks, at the store he was as cordial and flirtatious to her as he was to everyone, but so different on Aunt Helen's dock, her porch, on the glider, on the daybed inside.

But on their last night together, after eating the Ciardi family casserole, prepared by Lou in Aunt Helen's kitchen as Carole looked on, neither made mention of anything beyond that evening. Of all the things they had talked about, saying good-bye was not one. But on the porch, early in the morning, Lou said good-bye, said that in her face, he saw family and home.

"You look different," Gary had said at dinner the day she returned, after the kids had gone their separate ways.

First, it was the small things they didn't agree on, which brand of tuna to buy or what to have for dinner. Then, they didn't agree on Kate and boys, or the boys and sports, on what color to paint the bathrooms, on whether to hire someone to remodel the bathroom or tackle it themselves.

As their inability to compromise grew, Friday dinner preparations became a chore. Carole had to remind Gary to stop for bread and often she selected new merlots and Australian wines over his preferred Chianti.

Gary began working late. Carole started going to bed sometimes before he came home. Even the casserole, several times prepared as a peace offering, no longer got its fair share of either accolades or criticisms.

Through all this, Carole would find herself at the pantry, and at the refrigerator and at the freezer making certain she always had the ingredients for the casserole, making certain there would always be food, no matter what.

If Gary had suspected something, she would never know for sure. But what other reason for his abrupt leaving? It wasn't like him to share hurt, sorrow, grief. If he told the story of why he left his family after twenty-three years, it would be revealing to all of them, perhaps himself included. Carole was left thinking about the lure of another woman, one more suited to his growing quiet, a woman who could be happy wondering, rather than knowing.

Her skin prickled every time she considered he might have found out.

Way in the back of her mind, behind the hurt, Carole felt she probably deserved what had happened. But certainly what had happened at the lake, certainly it was not enough, on its own, to destroy a marriage, and those things that surround it.

That Gary might have had a reason for leaving would never occur to the children, at least Carole didn't think so. And it was he who left them, even though they were nearly adults, left the house, left her, and he was silent about why.

When Gary announced he was leaving, she thought she had said, "What?" and "Why?" but she was not sure. Somehow, she had been ready for this, waiting for this.

That night, after he left, she had made the casserole. She made it the traditional way, the way she had hundreds of times, the way the family most preferred it. The word "family" stuck in her mind as she grated the cheese for the topping. Was it still family if the father was gone? If the mother had been unfaithful? Who would tell the kids? She lit a candle and poured some wine. The casserole bubbling in the oven was the loudest sound in the house.

As she put on the Joni Mitchell CD and poured herself a second glass, she realized the children were coming home from college in ten days, Kate first, then the boys. She and Gary had to have a plan by then, of what to say, what to do, of how to portray the future.

The oven timer beeped and for a while she let it. She welcomed a sound that required an action, something she had to do. But as the timer's intermittent beep became irritating, she snapped it off, and removed the dish from the oven.

The familiar fragrance filled the kitchen and the cheese was a golden brown just like always, but she took a bite and the onion tasted bitter. Another bite revealed the peppers too crisp, too raw, the pasta too soft, the spices not just right. But the sausage, the heat was there, alone trying to make the casserole successful, alone trying to make the effort worthwhile.

The Pasta Maker

T he coffee maker stood ready, its reservoir full, its filter loaded with finely ground dark breakfast blend, the auto-brew ready to snap on, signaling the beginning of a new day.

Last night, Claudia had prepared it. Remembering at the last moment, responding to its silent call, she'd walked into the darkened kitchen, feet bare on the cool tile floor. She got the coffee and the filter, then put them aside for a moment, while she reached for some ibuprofen and gulped two pills with a glass of water. She measured the coffee level to the top of the coffee scoop, just the way Robert preferred, because after all, he often said, if you didn't do it that way, how could there be any coffee consistency at all. She hesitated briefly, contemplating adding one extra scoop, anticipating the brouhaha tomorrow when the coffee would be too strong, when the coffee maker might have to silently take the blame. But she added just the required amount of fresh ground beans—no more, no less—and slammed the top of the coffee maker closed.

Now it was morning and the fragrance of the brewing coffee surrounded her as she rolled her shoulders and stretched her arms in an attempt to get her body moving. She fluffed her black hair and pulled it briefly into a ponytail, then let it fall loosely down her back. All this she did while moving gracefully to the kitchen window. Her thin cotton robe blew lightly in the sea breeze. She opened the window as wide as it would go.

She felt the beach house needed the fresh air to maintain the delicate coexistence of the members of this household. Sometimes in the early morning, the sea air made her think of the galleys of ships on the high seas where an oak container accommodated a block of ice to keep things cool, and the tin coffee pot was on the open fire. It was a time when there had been no connecting current uniting stove and refrigerator and coffee maker. It was a time when people paid more attention to each other and less attention to things.

It was quiet now. Robert and the children were still sleeping, giving her a reprieve from the whining, complaining and criticism they all could heap her way. Her kids were young, eight and ten, and a certain amount of that was expected. Besides, their engaging innocence mostly overshadowed their negative side. Robert was different, his teenage daughters, too, so demanding and critical of just about everything.

Claudia rested her elbows on the sink and leaned forward to take a cleansing breath. As she glanced down, a long piece of dried pasta stuck to the sink brought the previous evening's debacle to mind once again. They needed a pasta maker, he had said. She knew that meant eventually they would add one to the dissonant choir of appliances that hummed, cranked, ground and perked noises in her kitchen, their kitchen, his kitchen.

That piece of spaghetti will just have to stay there, she thought, remembering all the cleanup she had done the night before. It had been too sticky anyway, underdone and too starchy. If he liked it that way, he should be the one to clean it up—she would consider it a step in the right direction if he would even notice it. She sighed.

Last night there had been arguments over the garlic, one clove or two, minced or crushed, his way or hers, arguments louder than they had had for a while. After the decision to use two cloves crushed, Robert had prepared dinner with elegance as always, pasta al dente, too raw for her, and sauce piquant, too spicy for everyone but him. From the bakery in the seaside village, he had selected bread with garlic chunks and onion pieces baked on the crust, too garlicky and oniony for the kids. Maybe buy a loaf of plain bread too next time, she had said. It will just be easier. Life isn't easy, he had replied calmly. Life isn't easy, he said again, looking at the kids, maybe thinking about the adjustments both families still were trying to make. She sighed again.

Almost two years ago, she had found Robert wandering in the world, surrounded by gadgets and things he could control with switches and buttons.

His power was great then, at a time when hers was weak. Loneliness and single parenthood were sapping her energies. Her former husband had drained her bank account while she stood passively by, as she often had during their years together. On the day she met Robert, she had dragged herself, against all of her good judgment, out of the office for a solitary lunch in the sun, a fair maiden in great distress. Robert's high-end watch glinting in the noonday sun caught her attention as she sat eating a pita with tuna, lettuce and tomato on the stone wall circling the fountain near the office building where she worked. Then his watch beeped, warning him of something impending and she smiled.

Obviously irritated at the reminder, he looked up to see her smiling, and smiled, too. Then he stood up straighter, brushed back the gray-flecked hair that fell over one eye and adjusted the French cuffs of his shirt under his black doubled-breasted blazer. He sat down next to her. Not a cloud in the sky, he said, though he hadn't seemed particularly happy about it. But all she could see was a good—no—great looking stranger actually paying her some attention. It was male interest from someone other than her co-workers in the insurance office whose attention seemed always to verge on sexual harassment. This was a first in her year of aloneness and it was exciting. A white-collar man was what she thought she wanted, not the blue-collar-dirty-fingernail type she had already had quite enough of. If she had been paying attention, she would have seen that even though this stranger's fingernails shone with the subtleties of a good manicure, the shine obscured the wrinkles in his brow caused by repeated furrowing when things did not go his way.

In the weeks and months after meeting at the fountain, she had overlooked other signs of potential trouble, as well. Later on, in his condescending manipulation of waiters, valets and salespeople wherever their developing relationship took them, there were more signs that she ignored. She so wished not to be alone, not to be in charge, not to be responsible, that she let him have it all, just as he desired, not realizing what she would lose—not at first.

She didn't see herself standing in his summer place on the Jersey shore, in a gleaming black-and-white, state-of-the-art kitchen, surrounded by three different kinds of ovens, and a state-of-the-art knife sharpener. She didn't hear herself silently shrieking that she was not one of his gadgets, that she couldn't be turned off and on with a switch, that she wouldn't be powered up by a stronger battery. She only felt herself nestled in strong arms, comforted by a man's warmth, taken care of in most ways by this elegant, no-nonsense man.

On their third date, Robert had cooked a fabulous gourmet meal, her very favorite, salmon en croute. She had meant to ask, but then had forgotten, the questions on the tip of her tongue. Could he accept the occasional need for canned ravioli? Would he welcome the comfort of the quick and easy meal, while other more important, kid-related matters received their due?

And last night, more chinks in the armor had emerged. His children were out with their summer acquaintances, affording him the privacy he was accustomed to, but her children were there, always there, and required some attention she was usually glad to give. But last night they were grousing, starting already with complaints about the planned seafood pasta feast, a meal they couldn't care less for. She shushed their plaintive requests to eat a pizza on the deck, recognizing that even at their young age they realized the value of their absence, and they tiptoed around Robert's preparations for the evening meal. They'd never been big seafood fans, she had made known in several different ways.

His one real joy, she had observed over their past year together, was preparing meals. It was his way, she supposed, of nurturing himself and his family. His joy in cooking was one of the things she had taken pride in for her choice of a second husband. It was a trait that when discussed with female acquaintances, drew jealous laughter, not to mention comparisons where other men always fell short.

She had also observed that Robert did not push buttons gently, or place tops on securely, or wash things carefully.

It was all done with a rough, quick hand. He saved his gentle touch for garnishing the plates with ostentatious, tiny spiced apples and tufts of purple lettuce.

He did take some care with her. He could be wonderfully gentle and warm and understanding. It just was not always his first inclination.

Her sighs addressed Robert's impatience, the way he yelled at the teenagers to do their jobs, the way they half-did everything since their mother had left. They said it was quieter now without their mother's strident orders, requiring everyone to hop to, to cook, clean and polish for her associates, her business partners, her friends invited to the beach house for a working holiday. Everything and everyone had been tense all the time.

Claudia watched the clouds move in over the bay. The gray horizon turned darker as the clouds became actual rain and moved closer to the coastline, pelting the waves. This looks like a day full of rain, she thought, remembering the forecast. We need a plan.

She absently wiped some dust off the top of the coffee maker. The water pumping from the reservoir made a swishing sound she associated with the start of a new day. Maybe today will be the day we all click, she thought. The first five days of their two-week stay already had been less than restful, wasted on bickering and the selfishness that his side brought to the relationship. She opened the door to the deck and willed the coffee maker to hurry so she could have some coffee-drinking time on the deck, by herself. It seemed to oblige, swishing more fervently, the fragrance stronger. She lovingly patted its top, like a pet, after she poured her white ceramic mug full, the mug from her former life that she couldn't give up, the one that said "single and loving it."

She pulled the robe more tightly to her and stepped onto the deck. The breeze had become wind and it was cool and refreshing and clear. Her hair blew across her face and she closed her eyes in enjoyment of the moment.

After a few sips, she had a plan. She would separate them all today, hoping that a few hours apart would make them more cordial to each other at dinner later. That night, they could share their experiences. She would take her kids to the outlet malls and let them run around for a bit while she bought a pasta maker. A gadget gift for Robert was always good, especially if it was something he could play with. Yes, it was a good plan. She closed her eyes again, against the rain now pelting her face; sharp stinging raindrops commanding attention, big wet splotches on her thin robe. Time to go inside.

Her plan, suggested over breakfast, was met with relief. She could tell her children looked forward to being just the three of them, his children looked forward to being without her family. She knew Robert looked forward to being with just his daughters. There was relaxation in the air as they all went their separate ways, agreeing to meet at the house at five o'clock.

Claudia and her children arrived at the mall in a downpour. They skipped through puddles, laughing at their wet feet and soaking tee shirts. They shook themselves like dogs under the protection of the store roof overhangs and enjoyed a fast food lunch at the food court, ending with hot chocolate chip cookies. All the questions that she wanted to ask about their happiness seemed an intrusion into their fun. Her son dragged them into the sports stores. Her daughter dragged them into the lingerie outlet, embarrassing her brother and surprising her mother with a request for her first bra. Then, it was nearly time to go and Claudia reminded them they just needed to get the pasta maker. The children, anticipating more unwanted pasta dinners, tried to deter her. They were tired, they said. They had to go to the bathroom. But she would not waver, giving them any number of unacceptable reasons why the purchase was necessary.

At the appliance store, she went directly to the counter and asked for the most expensive pasta maker, the one with the most options, the largest manual, anything that would indicate   preeminence in its field. Carrying the carton to the car was difficult. It was heavy and bulky and added to her other purchases, definitely a burden. It bumped around in the trunk as she turned corners and braked in stop-and-go traffic.

They arrived home first, and even though they were alone, whispered about how to best present this great surprise. Her son said to wrap it and present it formally after dinner, but her daughter wanted to take it out of the box and set it on the table just to see what Robert would do. Claudia agreed. They carefully removed it from the white foam packing and set it on the kitchen table, propping up the accompanying directions and cookbook. Just as they finished topping it with a huge red bow, they heard the others arriving. They scurried to sit nonchalantly in the living area, pretending to work on their summer puzzle.

Hearing angry, arguing voices and the rustling of bags, she had a sinking feeling.

"The red swimsuit looked better," Robert's older daughter pouted.

"I told you ten times there wasn't enough of it for the money," he snapped.

"Give it up," his other daughter said. "He's a geek and that's not going to change."

The younger children looked at each other, eyes wide and her son mouthed, "A geek?" Claudia didn't have time to comment before Robert snapped again, this time at her.

"I hope **your** afternoon wasn't full of listening to bickering and arguing like mine was," he snorted. "Or waiting outside of dressing rooms in every store. Or looking so many times at your watch that you finally lost count."

Claudia's skin flushed as she stood up.

"Shut up, all of you," she said. "I've had enough."

She paused. "We had a great afternoon buying something special for you, Robert. But now I've changed my mind," she said slowly, emphasizing each word. "So go look in the kitchen and come and see what your gift **might have been**."

She ran into the kitchen, the rest following.

"I thought you would love it," she said to Robert, "but I haven't seen you love anyone or anything this week."

His eyes softened as he looked at the silver noodle machine with its wooden handle and ready instructions. Perhaps he was remembering his comment about a pasta maker last night, tossed at her in anger, and now here was this gift, so thoughtful and loving. He stepped forward to turn the crank but Claudia was quicker. She lifted his new toy off the table, strode out the door onto the deck and hurled it off into the sand and rock below.

She leaned sobbing against the railing, and her children came running. They hugged her waist and whispered, "It's all right, Mommy."

Robert came and put his arms around her, and the children made room for him. His daughters, for once speechless, stood behind her, their fingertips touching her shoulders. For a moment, Robert and the girls and her children were linked through her, connected with a current

97

stronger than electrical, requiring no cords, as they stood looking down at the pasta maker, watching its six-inch dough roller still bouncing down the rocks toward the sea. They saw its fancy wood grip handle twirling down the sand, its easy-lock dough roller adjustment dial and removable double cutter for spaghetti and fettuccine mangled against the hard stone.

Gazpacho

Their long-awaited weekend at the Toronto International Film Festival started happily. No magic, but Justine thought that after being together for two years, this is what it must be like to settle down, to be married. Back home in Buffalo, they shared their mutual passion for movies in comfortable silence on the couch. There were occasional phone calls at work to discuss household matters that had gone unmentioned the previous evening. And sex when they weren't too tired, physically or emotionally. She, leaning on the kitchen counter, would chatter about her day, and Paul would listen, as he took charge of dinner, giving her direction about what she could do to help. Preparing meals was the thing that always made her feel the most connected to Paul, that they were in sync.

In the kitchen, they moved around each other with ease, never even brushing elbows unless one of them wanted to get the other's attention, just like that scene close to the happy ending in *Working Girl*, where Harrison Ford and Melanie Griffith are in the world's smallest kitchen, sharing the same piece of toast and drinking coffee as they pack each other's lunches with an intimacy that only could come from having survived chaos together.

It was under Paul's direction she had begun to enjoy cooking; previously it had been just a necessity that she had never thought of in conjunction with the word "enjoy." And she did enjoy the man who cooked, who wanted to make love in the afternoon, who cared about things like laundry detergent. It hadn't mattered so much that, for all of the great activities he enjoyed, talking wasn't one of them, really talking about what they wanted, what they were thinking, what they liked about each other, about anything. But food and cooking it, he could talk about that.

It was the middle of their long weekend at the festival and they'd seen a variety of films, both independent and foreign. They had made their selections carefully from the large online festival catalog, as they sat in front of the laptop in their Euro-style dining area over a light meal of bruschetta and portobello mushroom appetizers. They made certain all the films would have some zest or flavor, so it was no accident that most of them involved food. Their choices ranged from period pieces, where people ate sumptuous fare as they made innocent yet seductive comments and shared veiled eye contact in the true repressed spirit of Jane Austen, to modern films, with vineyards full of grapes and wines where people ate sumptuous fare as they made full body contact prone under the vines. So, yet again, food was the focus of their entertainment, even though they were in a cosmopolitan city in another land, albeit just across the border.

They had a movie to see at one o'clock that afternoon, an Italian Indie triptych of stories about love, and Justine was looking forward to a sensuous few hours. After waiting in the customary long line, they found seats in the theater and were quickly absorbed into the relationship difficulties of very attractive, very thin Italian men and women in different time periods; one film set in the 19th century, one in the 20th, and one in a not easily discernible period of time, perhaps the future.

There was laughter. There were tears. There was much skin-to-skin contact and many sensual little touches like wiping wine from lips with thumbs. There were long caresses and lots of Italian terms of endearment, although the subtitles seemed much too short for what the actors actually were saying. As they left, she was moved to buy the movie CD full of soft jazz tunes, some happy, some sad, but all evoking freedom and sunshine and vineyards and the general cachet of foreign lands.

Justine sometimes wondered whether, if she had known during that film what she learned a few hours later, it would have looked the same to her.

They went to an après film restaurant and settled into a corner booth covered in leather—smooth, soft, sensuous. They ordered wine, big globe goblets, shining in the candlelight. The restaurant's menu was foreign sounding and exciting. Paul ordered a lobster ravioli appetizer. Justine chose the gazpacho.

It doesn't get much better than this, she remembered thinking as the waiter poured the deep red wine. For Justine, there was always a moment of serenity when the waiter poured and the only sound was the gurgling of the liquid, the only action a breathless waiting for the first whiff of the grape. She was enjoying that moment intensely when Paul started talking. It was not his smooth Paul voice, but someone whose voice broke, who stuttered, whose eyes could not meet hers.

"Justine," he began. He even reached for his goblet with a jerky motion and took a few big gulps. "This isn't good."

"What isn't good about it?" she asked. She held her glass high and looked for pieces of cork or anything that would negate Paul's pleasure in his wine selection. Then, through the top of her goblet, she saw that a glimmer of the irritation she recently had seen on Paul's face had reappeared.

"Not this. Not the wine. It's us that isn't good."

Like an animal whose senses were heightened at an approaching danger, suddenly Justine could smell the perfume of the woman next to them, something spicy with a hint of citrus. Now, she actually heard the background music, soft jazz, the score from some movie, she remembered. Maybe Jeff Bridges was in it. And some blonde.

As she put down her goblet, she noticed Paul's hair, curling in the heat of the early fall, more gray strands than she remembered. Then his eyes, brown and alert, darting around the room, not looking at her as he spoke. Then his nose, small for a man. She watched his mouth, more closely than she ever had.

"I may be an excellent cook," he was saying, "but I'm not a brave man." He stopped as though she might disagree, but then continued. "Rather than create the meal of a lifetime for you at home, and then tell you I need to move on, I thought it better to avoid a scene and tell you now over a less than memorable meal. I need to get this off my chest so I—so we—can enjoy the rest of the meal—and the festival, of course."

She wondered how he could not know that whatever meal he dumped her at would be a memorable meal. The more he talked, the quieter she got, and an observant man, someone who was thinking at all about the woman he was in the process of casting aside, might have noticed that. He was saying something about how it wasn't her, it was him.

How he had difficulty seeing himself with one person for a long time. That two years was longer than he had been with anyone, as if that should make her feel special. It was like using the same recipe for beef bourguignon over and over again, he explained. Didn't she understand? Wasn't she feeling the same way?

She didn't and she wasn't.

She was still struggling to understand the full impact of what he had said as the waiter brought their food. Paul was talkative now, positively glib with relief. He talked about the film they had seen, about their film choices for tomorrow as though there were no earth-shattering difference between them. He spoke so casually that Justine wondered if she had imagined the previous several minutes.

Paul quickly dispatched his ravioli, stopping once to ask if she wanted a taste. She shook her head, spooned her gazpacho gently. It was spicy and perfectly chilled. Paul asked for a taste. Normally she would have extended her spoon for him but now she gestured for him to use his own. He looked at her oddly, then scooped up some of the spicy liquid.

He said. "Not quite there."

"What exactly is 'there'?" she asked.

"There needs to be a complexity. This tastes too simple," he said.

"How does a soup taste simple? Or complex for that matter?"

"Pardon me," said the man at the table to their right. "I can answer that."

His companion touched his arm, but he continued.

"A simple taste would present an obvious flavor—like tomato, and that means more tomato than anything else. Or if you are making an asparagus bisque, more asparagus than anything else." The man's voice was convincing, soothing, conversational with the tiny quirks of a Canadian accent.

"A complex taste makes you lick your lips in wonderment. There is a tang or mystery to the flavor, one you must decipher. The essence of gazpacho is complexity made simple." Now the man's voice was enthusiastic. He was bald in that very hip way of being bald, and had glasses, black rims so thin they were barely discernible around the lenses. He wore his gray fitted silk shirt with the sleeves rolled up.

Justine and Paul both stared at him as he swirled the gazpacho in his own dish, then tasted.

"This soup, you are correct," he looked at Paul. "It isn't there."

A food critic, Justine thought, and a pretty brash one at that, to insinuate himself into their break-up dinner. However, his words were making her think about taste and complexity and Paul.

"That was interesting," Paul whispered. "Talk about dinner table eavesdropping ... probably a food critic; they think they know it all."

But Justine had moved past the bald man's comments. The odd thing was, as she continued eating, two things were happening. One, Paul was chatting and she was silent. And two, all the men in the room had moved into focus. This was a surprising development as Justine was not, had not been, an avid watcher of men, had not, in two years, considered anyone else as relationship material. The bald man had grabbed her attention and her taste was heightened, her palate alive, taste buds alert. For the first time she cared about complexity. She pushed away her bowl, soup half-eaten. She felt positively European doing that, an American brought up to eat everything on her plate.

The waiter, Nordic, long hair, blond, blue-eyed, had an aura like the first cool breeze of autumn as he hurried by their table, then came back to clear their dishes.

"Finished?" He looked at her bowl and then at her.

She nodded and felt Paul's dismay at not being offered what remained. Why should they still share food as they teetered on the verge of not sharing anything else? Yesterday, sharing leftovers was romantic. Now it would feel like eating garbage.

But one good thing was true as she grasped for something positive; to her, the gazpacho had been marvelous. In fact, she felt if she could enjoy it during this surreal moment in her life, it must be magical. As it did in *Like Water for Chocolate*, perhaps food did have magical qualities and could manipulate emotions.

And now she remembered that making their own gazpacho was one thing they had not done together, but it was the thing they had promised each other to do time and again. Someday I'll teach you, he'd say. The family recipe. The first time he said it, she had thought, "Aren't you Swedish?" but she hadn't mentioned it.

Paul waved his hand for the check.

Justine wondered why it was when you think you will never see someone again, you remember the small things and they seem so big. Like the way he prepared the kitchen back home. He chopped onion and garlic, the onion pieces chopped evenly to size, just this side of diced. His hands moved swiftly, competently, and the garlic was minced just right as well. Oh, the fragrance of those vegetables as they sweated, yes, that was the precise word, in their high-end saucepan. She would watch as they grew warm and small beads of fragrant vegetable sweat oozed to the surface. He allowed the vegetables to sweat, like they themselves did after a good workout, when they would forgo the shower at the health club, get in the car and race to the apartment, sweaty and hot for each other. Paul's hands were deft, knowing, pleasing, like Johnny Depp's hands as he makes perfect love to a perfect stranger in the opening sequence of *Don Juan DeMarco*.

There had been two years of exercising, making love, of cooking instruction, all of which she had willingly entered into. But now, now she was worried that, despite all she had learned, she would never be Julia Child to his Jacques Pepin.

Because she didn't know what else to do, she went with him to the ten o'clock film, their last for that day, but later she would not even remember the title of that film, so desperate was she for an idea, any idea, for a way out of this trouble. No matter what scenes were playing out on the screen, her mind jumped from scene to scene in their relationship.

She remembered the many times they had trekked together to the public market, arms around each other, joined at the hip. She saw them together shaking the melons, then they would move on to vegetables. He touched them all differently and with a reverence. The tomatoes, red and smooth as silk, onions with their sweet and pungent smell, and the cucumbers, some deep green and waxy, others knotted and bumpy like alligator skin.

He was a brilliant food-and-cooking risk-taker. Following a recipe down to the last grain of salt was her style. She even owned a set of measuring spoons labeled a dash and a pinch—a gift from Paul—and she used them, perhaps a joke to him, but not to her. To her it was an acknowledgment of understanding and his acceptance of a foible.

And later, at home, combining these ingredients for a dinner by candlelight, his chicken parmesan was incredible. Her chocolate cake, however, was superior, and if he knew she had used a mix with a few ad-ons, he never let on. She had loved him for overlooking that.

And then, in the darkened theater, sometime just before she began imagining life without him, and somewhere between the breakup and the tearful reunion of characters in the ten o'clock film, Justine had an epiphany. The gazpacho. She would make it for him. After all, the soup needed complexity and the way she felt now, there would be plenty of it. She would make it and something would happen, she was sure of it.

So in the next few weeks, she did her research. She went online whenever she could, usually at work on her lunch hour, but also at home since Paul was living elsewhere now. And she learned many things. She learned that gazpacho had started out as a use for old bread and originally it was poor people's food—stale bread, water and olive oil with some tomatoes and other vegetables all pounded together into a paste in a wooden bowl, then finished with a dash of vinegar.

She learned that the soup should have texture and discernible vegetable bits, not be a pureed mush. She found that when it came to gazpacho, there were fresh tomato devotees, skinless tomato enthusiasts, herb aficionados, tad-of-wine advocates, and vinaigrette zealots. All these were over the top and talked much more about the process than the result, in her opinion. The most memorable and romantic thing she discovered was that it should be served chilled on a hot day and preferably within sight of the sea. She would capture it. Her soup was going to be amazing.

It had been a month since the evening they returned from the festival and Paul had packed his things and hugged her and left, talking about remaining friends. And tonight she had invited him for dinner under the auspices of the friendship he thought they could continue.

First, she set up the counter as Paul had taught her, utensils arranged to the left of the cutting board. Then, looking at the gleaming paring knives, the gourmet cutlery and the small prep bowls within reach of her left hand, she moved everything over to the right-hand side. She reached for the tomatoes she had placed in the ceramic dish, not in the basket he favored. She started cutting and the knife slid easily through the tomato skin, one-half to one-quarter inch, just like Paul would insist. But Justine never had felt the pieces needed to be so uniform. She felt that some irregularity would add variety to the texture of the soup. She reached for the glass chopping board and the cucumbers and set about chopping them to her own specifications. Then the onions and celery. She hummed as she sliced and chopped and sieved. She stopped, wiped her hands and put on the soundtrack from that Italian film with the incredibly thin people. She swayed back and forth to jazz that was sometimes mournful, but more often exuberant, uninhibited. She put her vegetables in a solution of vinegar and spices, added some wine and poured herself some in one of the new globe goblets she had searched for and finally found at a little Italian grocery in the neighborhood.

Over the next few hours, the aroma of the marinating vegetables became exhilarating. That or the wine gave a feeling of well-being she hadn't experienced in several weeks. Whatever it was, when the doorbell rang, she was ready in her new off-the-shoulder gauze top and embroidered skirt. She imagined herself in the final scene of that Italian film, cavorting in a gauze peasant dress in the vineyards under the Italian sun, exhilarated, competent, full of confidence. The spiced scent of her new perfume was an invisible, delicate cloud around her. She started the music again and opened the door.

"Hi," Paul said. As he hugged her, the wine bottle he had brought bumped against her back. "What a surprise to get a dinner invite from you."

"I wanted to try a new recipe I found for gazpacho," she said.

"You have an old recipe?" Paul asked. He chuckled indulgently.

"You'd be surprised," Justine said. It was a comment delivered over her shoulder as she went to the kitchen to open the wine. First she took the soup from the refrigerator. As she removed the cover, the fragrance was intoxicating. It was dizzying, and as she put her hand on the counter to steady herself, she felt, really felt, the growing complexity.

Paul had followed her into the kitchen. He closed his eyes for a moment, leaned over the bowl and breathed deeply. When he opened his eyes, she saw surprise and desire. Their eyes met, and she felt a familiar warmth. She thought that if this soup had started as poor people's food, now it was an investment. He reached for the wine bottle opener and deftly cut the protective wax and removed the cork.

"You look good," he said. "I like the outfit."

She took the cork from his hand and held it under her nose. "Nice," she said.

He poured the wine and Justine shivered with her usual anticipation at the sound of the liquid cascading into the goblet, at the first whiff of the wine.

"I've missed you doing that," he said. His voice was husky and he cleared his throat. "Hey, great wine glasses. Just like Toronto."

"You noticed."

"To something new," he said, handing her a glass.

"Yes."

They chatted about movies and their lives for a while. Then there was a silence, and Justine heard the music softly in the background.

"I just have to toss the salad and cut the bread," she said. She stood up and her skirt swirled. She'd never had a skirt that swirled before. She liked it.

"I'll help."

In her kitchen, formerly their kitchen, when she turned to put the cutting board on the counter, he was standing right in the way and she whacked his elbow.

"Sorry," she murmured.

As she reached into the drawer for the bread knife, he moved to the right to get the salad dressing carafe in the cupboard and stepped on her foot.

She winced.

"Are you okay?" he asked.

"I'm fine."

As he tossed the romaine and scattered the mesclun over it, she assembled the salad dressing she'd created, something new and piquant.

"Smells great. What's in it?" he said.

They both reached for the carafe and it started to tip. She rescued it and said, "Just see if you can guess when you taste it."

"Yes, let's just see," he said.

He went in the other room to pour more wine and she ladled the soup into the new tureen she'd found at an antiques store. The spices, the tomatoes, the cucumbers—

although blended, she could smell them all distinctly. This was complexity. And, she realized, a sign of something new.

"Smells incredible," he said.

"I know."

She smiled and served them both. Her skirt swirled as she moved around the table. Her peasant blouse dropped a bit off the shoulder as she held her glass out for more wine. Then she sat down across from the man who loved cooking, who liked to make love in the afternoon, who cared about laundry detergent, the man who was about to enjoy the world's most incredible gazpacho soup for the first, and last, time.

Pie Like No Other

At the county fair bake sale on that hot August day, Kenny thought, without bias, that Felicia's French apple pie stood out like the brightest star in a galaxy of delectable pastries. It could have been the height of the crust or the tiny pastry leaves fluttering over the mound of golden dough. Maybe it was the scent of cinnamon or the secret spices that Felicia added. Whatever it was, Kenny couldn't remember ever wanting anything more than he wanted that pie that day in the blistering Ohio sun. He couldn't remember ever wanting anything less than the trouble he had now.

Kenny probably could've undone the other damage, had it not been for the night school class that he himself had encouraged Felicia to take. It wasn't that his wife was doing so well—she found it hard and frustrating. It generated many tears and much comforting, something that Kenny had started to like. That "silent man" routine his Uncle Herb had talked about loud and long on his parents' front porch on cool summer evenings hadn't worked at all in Kenny and Felicia's marriage. Kenny had learned that quickly as he fended off Felicia's flailing arms bent, it seemed, on pounding some comment out of him.

Felicia was different than the other women in Kenny's family. She was not accepting and silent about problems in family life. No, she was volatile and questioning and too damn friendly, especially in that night school class with that French Canadian guy, Yves. He should've known that was trouble when that name crept into her conversation.

"You know that cheese I told you about that I used to eat when I was small? Yves eats it and he feels like I do, that it tastes like home."

Then there was, "Oh, Yves loves that wine we took with us on our last apple trip," and Kenny wondered why their last apple trip together had come up in that conversation anyway. She got home late one night and it was because after class she and Yves had gone to his favorite coffee place where they served beignets, a word Kenny had never even heard. He almost wished she would be silent, not share this information because it is often, no almost always, true that what you don't know won't hurt you.

Kenny thought himself competitive in the looks department and he felt he was a good provider. Right after the wedding three years back, right after they both had celebrated their twenty-third birthdays, they had moved into the first floor apartment of an old house in the southern Ohio town where he grew up. The address was 23 Stetson Street, a lucky number and a perfect street name by Kenny's thinking. Felicia fixed it up real nice with her southern Louisiana Cajun taste, a little French thing here and one there, lots of red and white. And when she wondered if she should go to school, he said hell yes, and even got her the course list on a special trip to the community college where he had gotten his associate's in accounting. This, in turn, had gotten him a job with a local accounting firm, which in turn left him time for rodeo— his first love after Felicia.

The smell of apples and spices drifted his way as he absently rubbed the back of his hand on the worn denim of his jeans. Sitting on the rough-hewn corral fence near the bake sale booth, he remembered how making one of those pies together had always been a glorious good time. He and Felicia would make a day of it several times each fall, leaving early on a Saturday with a picnic lunch. They would arrive at an orchard while the dew still clung to the fruits and pick two bushels of assorted apples, carefully placing them in the baskets to avoid bruising. Their hands would sometimes touch as they cradled the apples into their spots. With that touch they would look at each other and know something was right.

In the orchard they would find a spot in the shade and, just like in the French films Felicia had a passion for and Kenny pretended to love, they'd picnic on a red-and-white checked tablecloth with real china and crystal wine glasses. Felicia would always pack a French wine from the Normandy region and, while Kenny opened it, she would wait, pulling some strands of long blonde hair across her face like a veil, offering only a partial view of her deep red lips and lingering smile.

"Viens ici, Kenny," she'd beckon to him, using her night school French.

He would wait for her to play with the dark curls that escaped his wide-brimmed hat. This always made him feel desired. They'd lie innocently in each other's arms looking up through the trees at the blue cloudless sky until someone's stomach rumbled, reminding them it was way past lunchtime.

As Felicia unpacked cheese and bread, Kenny would look through their apples and choose a few for lunch. He always was amused by how some of their fruits resembled anatomical parts; a heart or a derriere, as Felicia would say.

They would eat, then head home, where Felicia wouldn't even have her jacket off before she began peeling the apples. Kenny's job was to unload the car and turn on the oven. He then would settle down with a beer at the kitchen table to watch Felicia create. She would utter French sounding words and grunts as she worked. The recipe was her Cajun grandmother's so Kenny supposed the French was an essential part of the process. Sometimes the grunting would make the hair on the back of his neck stand on end and make him short of breath with desire, but he knew nothing could interfere with this creation. Not until after the pie was in the oven could he touch her, even her hair; but then he could touch her wherever he wished for as long as he wanted.

Nothing gave a better feeling of well-being than their shared pie making, in which, as in much of their marriage, Kenny was content to take a back seat.

The trouble began when a few months earlier Felicia had given him the gift of a pie-making class at the community college.

"What the hell kind of gift is this?" he'd thundered. "I don't want to be baking any damn pies myself. I like the way you make the pies. The way we make the pies together."

"But we don't do it together," she'd said. "You always just sit there and watch me. You must be bored. I know you can do it, cheri. You could mix dough or peel apples."

"But I don't want to."

She said nothing, her second-generation Cajun eyes flashing, but they both knew something wasn't right.

And now, after several months completely devoid of pie making, Kenny badly wanted this pie, but he didn't dare buy it, because Felicia would somehow know. She'd get into some of her night school psychoanalytic crap about trying to buy her love when all he really wanted, he was sure, was the comfort of an apple pie. After three years of shared pie making, he deserved at least that.

When he had been in the army in Germany before the fast food burger franchises had made the leap across the Atlantic, Kenny had a buddy whose fiancée sent him a triple-stacked hamburger vacuum-packed in a special container. No greater love, Kenny had thought at the time. Now he wondered, if you vacuum-packed something, could you keep it forever? Could you do it to a pie? And, if you took a slice to a chemistry lab, could you have the spices analyzed so you could reconstruct the pie and sell it along with Felicia's secret family recipe?

God, he could see her face now as he handed her the finished pie along with a copy of the ingredients all wrapped up in a slick commercial wrapper labeled "Felicia's French Apple Pie." Her otherwise pale cheeks would develop red anger spots and her round kewpie doll mouth would pout rather than yell the way it really wanted to when she didn't get her way.

"Kenny," she'd begin, sidling up to him, her breasts trapping his arm. "You know that pie was our special thing, cheri. Why would you want to destroy all those good memories?"

But he wouldn't give in, not even when he could feel her breath on his neck and her generous hips against his.

As Kenny watched Felicia's Aunt Louisa in the booth, tidying up, moving pastries around so they would be tantalizingly displayed to lure the potential buyer, he thought about the irony of these past months. Felicia had been the one who was silent and Kenny the one trying to pry words from her, primarily words that would give him a clue to her feelings about still being with him.

Yes. He'd have to buy this pie and bring it home, he thought as he saw the sugar on the crust sparkle in the sun. When Felicia came home, she'd see it on their kitchen table and she'd know of his love for her and forget about that argument over the pie-baking course, cast all thoughts of Yves aside, and their life together would go on. He reached for his wallet. Not there. He patted all his pockets, shirt and jeans. Maybe in the car. He hopped off the fence and strode to the parking lot, dust kicking up on his cowboy boot heels.

As he walked, he thought about how he was so destined to have that pie, how just any buyer would not know all that went into a pie like that. Oh sure, the ingredients, sure, anyone might know that. But it required just the right amount of flour to encourage the chilled dough to roll just so on the pastry board. The light touch of the rolling pin covered with a pastry sleeve. The thin, raw dough baked into the golden crust. The lovingly sliced apples sprinkled and mixed with cinnamon, nutmeg, sugar and Felicia's secret, something else, something bitter, maybe lemon. But another buyer could not know the things that made this a pie like no other. No one else could know. Not even Yves.

But hey, Kenny realized as he found his wallet wedged into the driver's seat, he pretty much knew the ingredients, knew how to put it together, and could take a guess at how long to bake it. Hey, he thought as his boots crunched through the pebbled parking lot, past the midway and into the food court area, maybe he **could** make a pie all alone after all the times he'd watched and waited and been patient. Maybe Felicia was right. Maybe he should make one for her.

He felt lighter and happier than he had since the night they'd argued. He felt a torrent of goodwill toward everyone—Felicia, Aunt Louisa, even Yves—as he strode back toward the bake sale booth. He imagined he was having one of those epiphanies Felicia had been talking about, those moments where you learn something about yourself.

In his euphoria, he couldn't have imagined that at that very moment Felicia, her derriere round and firm like two ripe twenty-ounce apples, was walking away from the bake sale booth, carefully balancing her own apple pie-like-no-other in one hand, her new beignet cookbook in the other.

The Fortune Cookie

Lightning grabbed for the earth way in the distance, past the several groves of trees and bushes that surrounded the white colonial where they lived. You seldom saw the woman, but the man, Richard, was one of the original yard fanatics and you rarely saw him without some tool—a shovel, rake, clippers—like Edward Scissorhands, always with a gleaming steel appendage. And the cigarette was always there, too, hanging from his lip or pinched between two fingers with pale streams of smoke following him everywhere. Today, since it was a workday, there were no tools, only the cigarette accompanied by a cup of coffee. This early morning storm had his full attention, the lightning striking closer now, the rumbling of thunder following more and more quickly after each reaching flash.

You could almost see him mentally erecting a protective cover over his meticulously trimmed hedgerow, his newly planted seedlings, and the huge oak tree, his pride and joy. As the wind picked up, the lilac bush whipped against the house and the fragile columbine flailed in the hot, humid breeze. The sounds of the weather grew louder and Richard stopped on his way up the driveway to look at the heavens, his cigarette smoke creating a white pillar against the dark gray sky.

If anyone can make this stop, he can, you think, expecting him to raise his arms and command the storm to cease in a Moses-like gesture. You've observed that he is a man who gets what he wants. How else could he have a wife half his age, petite, soft-spoken and halting in her attempts to master his language, having left her native Norway to create a new life here with him?

Because your thoughts are those of a woman newly alone, replaced by someone younger, different, new, you speculate that somehow she calculated their first encounter. You don't consider that she may have been young and lonely, and looking for love, or that he might have frightened her at first, that his power as a man, particularly an American man, was immense.

Your idle mind, stimulated by morning caffeine, creates their meeting at an outdoor Chinese restaurant on one of the fjords that must exist in Oslo. He is at an important meeting with some Chinese clients who have traveled to Oslo for an economic summit. There also is an interpreter, and they all bow politely to the tall American in the dark business suit. They drink green tea, brewed at their table from fresh tea leaves.

She arrives and sits alone at a table close to the water. As the men drink tea and talk business, they seem to notice nothing else, so engrossed are they in the business of business and of money. However, as the men eat and continue to talk, Richard becomes aware of her. She is sitting only a few tables away, waiting still for something or someone. Soon he finds he cannot concentrate on interest rates and loan conditions. He can see only her ankles crossed demurely, her hands gripping the teacup. Her thick blonde hair frames a pale, delicate face. The power of her innocence is immense. Then he meets her eyes, wide and dark, and detects a tentative smile in his direction. He is flattered and to the consternation of his companions, he excuses himself and strides to her table. They exchange a few words, a business card, a hotel address and he returns, now focused. He knows she will call. He feels it.

You imagine that for a moment, she doesn't know what to do as she sits by the water, now that the man is aware of her and she of him. She wants to leave but cannot, and orders more tea and some cookies. The waiter presents her with a dish of small sweet almond cakes, square lemon-flavored biscuits and a fortune cookie. She reaches for the fortune cookie. If fortune smiles, she will take the path; if it doesn't, she will toss his card into the fjord.

The cookie is crisp. She breaks it in two and it does not crumble. The tiny bit of paper falls to the plate. She takes it and reads: "It is worth it to take a chance." She decides then to make the call, even with broken English, and she does that evening, not brazenly but timidly, so sweetly that the man wonders briefly about the wisdom of even meeting her. But he does. They meet and for a week, for the rest of his stay, even though in his polite touches and in her shy, soft conversation there are rumblings of a storm, they meet innocently, except for the last evening when they are overwhelmed by the miles that are about to come between them. They give in to each other, reacting to a tempest of desire, not thinking about her youth and his age or innocence and experience or family or wife or children. That tempest continues across land and across oceans for months, through the miracles of cellphone, email and even fax machine and perhaps it was email that finally got action, as Richard's wife read the words from Norway that he may or may not consciously have left on the screen: "It is worth it to take a chance."

123

From your front porch sipping your coffee, you watch Richard as you have on many mornings. You can accept how she could find him attractive, but to see how they could be together requires all the stereotypes you can dredge up from Hollywood movies and pulp fiction—that perhaps young European women crave father figures, that they respect their elders, that they curry the favor of affluent Americans. But you think perhaps that is not fair. After all, he is attractive, tall and lean, lines of age forming in ways kind to his chiseled cheeks and jaw, his eyes blue, bright blue, his thick hair more gray now than when you first became neighbors. She is small and quiet, choosing American styles, shorts and tank tops, blonde hair cropped short. Her accent still is so heavy even after the ten years they've been together that you wonder how he understands anything she says.

You find it funny that after all these years of living so close, you never wondered about the two of them, never thought much about how they came together, until recently, until you were suddenly alone. Now you wonder how his former wife and teenage children reacted when he came back from a trip to Europe with the declaration that he had found a different woman, someone with new and different ways of doing almost everything, someone younger with more energy who barely spoke his language in words, maybe only in gestures and actions and maybe best in the dark.

You wonder for the millionth time how it happens, how men are lured away, what the warning is, if there is time to take cover. The thought of it angers you once again but you focus on Richard, in your mind seeing him raise his arms to make all storms disappear.

In the evenings, different fragrances waft across the street: fish, cheeses, and fresh baked rye bread replacing meatloaf, pork chops and chocolate cake. Lives and meals are different now but you think he must still prefer chocolate cake to the faint lemon taste of fortune cookies. You wonder if they buy them. You wonder does she ever make them. You even wonder if she writes her own fortunes and slips them inside.

You remember that when you open a fortune cookie it always crumbles, how the tiny fortune sometimes falls in the remnants of the meal on your plate. When you fish it out, covered with lobster sauce or whatever else you have eaten, it's never exciting. It always sounds like something the wise and often-mocked Confucius would say, not something risky, something inviting intrigue, something that would change the path of life as you know it, not something that would ever steer you toward another man.

A sharp crack of thunder and the crackling of electricity bouncing off the earth pulls your attention back to Richard, still in the driveway, his T-shirt now pasted to his chest by wind and rain, his curly hair flattened to his head, khaki shorts sticking to vigorously muscled legs. He refuses to go in. He is as fascinated by the storm as you are by him, a man who would disrupt everything, create havoc in a family, risk it all—job, children, home—for a new beginning at the half-century mark. What makes it worth it, you try to understand as the wind and stinging rain finally drive you from the porch into the house.

What you do understand as she comes out on their porch, her eyes looking for him as she glides down the driveway and slips her arm around his waist, as his arm circles her shoulders and they hold each other tight in the driving rain of this early morning turbulence—what you do understand is that he's not the only one who got what he wanted.

125

Wedding Cake

I t wasn't the way he thought their marriage would begin, he wiping ganache from his face with his best man's linen napkin, she giggling uncontrollably, even after their promises to be civilized at the cake table. Mark had grabbed the napkin and dabbed at the creamy chocolate. He hadn't been able to look at Jacqueline. People have since said her face was playfully impish, some said devilish, others hadn't noticed. The only clue, he had heard her laugh softly as his hand folded over hers, holding the cake knife, just the way the wedding planner lady had demonstrated at the rehearsal, all this amid Jacqueline's mild protestations that this was her second time and she knew the drill.

He remembered how at that cake table, five years ago today, he had experienced a frightening moment of doubt. But doesn't everyone have doubts, he had thought? How can you be sure she's the one? The angel on his left shoulder closest to his heart had said, "Forgive her," but the devil perched on his right shoulder had questions. "What's she thinking? Did you not agree to no cake smashing? What the hell?"

There was more. He and Jacqueline had planned the wedding together—ordered the food, flowers, chosen the church, interviewed and been interviewed by the pastor, and then had edited and agreed on their vows, at least the first draft, in a coffee shop in New Bedford, Massachusetts, in the spring. He had written that draft, using the skills he had developed in college as a technical writer and in his former jobs working in corporate communications and doing freelance work. But until the day of the ceremony, she had forgotten to tell him she had slightly rewritten the vows that they had agreed to use. She had omitted the word "obey" from the old New England tried-and-true traditional liturgy they had chosen, and added the word "cherish." He might have found it a tender moment, if they had discussed it earlier. After all, people were all about making the service their own. And, obedience was not something he expected from a mate and felt the reverse should also be true. So she wanted it removed, said it was not a word that was used that much anymore. So big deal. But he would have enjoyed knowing about the change at least the day before. He had no chance to ask her the why of it. What in her life or experience prompted her to want that particular word substitution, he wondered. It might have been a telling moment. So, on his wedding day, for the first time in this relationship, Mark had experienced a vaguely uncomfortable feeling that he recognized as fear of commitment, and he wasn't sure whose.

On that spring day by the harbor, only the cake had caused discord. On the coffee shop veranda overlooking the ocean, Jacqueline, ever the businesswoman, had looked to the spreadsheet on her laptop and noticed the decision on the cake hadn't been made.

After Mark had begun to share his research on the matter of cakes, which was considerable since, as he said, he was a writer and interested in symbolism of many kinds, she said that she preferred simply to think of the

128

cake as a palate-sweetening thing that people could look forward to either because the reception was nearly all over and they could leave, or because maybe they would see something fun or interesting or—in some cases—hostile. Then her eyes had twinkled.

It was then he had said that cake smashing had no place in their relationship.

She had said, "Oh really?" and smiled.

He saw the smile and he told her he was serious, that the cake had meaning and in fact, sweetness was part of it—the sweetness of the union, an abundance of joy. It was all symbolic. And weddings were all about symbolism.

Okay then, we'll have chocolate, she had said, because everyone likes it and it's tasty.

He maintained chocolate was ordinary, everyday, a birthday and dessert staple. Ordinary. He asked if she thought tasty was what a wedding cake should be. She sat back in her chair and said she liked chocolate and asked if that made her ordinary. Said it was her favorite. And asked if that meant she was super ordinary.

He asked her to think about symbolism. Think about white cake—for faith and purity—the essence of the marital relationship. Or spice, representing the excitement of two people becoming one. Or marble cake, possibly mirroring the merging of two souls as they join together. He said white cake was his personal favorite.

A man with a heart of a poet, she had sighed, making a column in the spreadsheet for the word "cake."   And murmured, how did I ever find you.

After a few moments of looking out over the water with her arms folded in front of her, she had said that their compromise cake had to be spice. She had held her cup in the air and said they should toast to this, the first of many compromises. Their cups had touched and she had laughed.

She had pulled her dark hair back behind one ear, the rest falling over her cheek. She had brown eyes and a mouth capable of quick outbursts as well as thoughtful words, and great passion. At thirty-seven years old, he had felt he had waited a long time to make this choice and he had loved many things about her—her passion, her intelligence, her spontaneity.

But looking back, spice cake had not been a compromise; it had been a settling. To agree to either chocolate or white, for one of them to give in a bit, that would have been the compromise. Cooperate, negotiate, concede, those were words that signified compromise. Not offering another absolutely unrelated solution. There was that and much else he had not seen, the shroud of love draped heavily over his eyes.

Spontaneity is overrated, he thought yet again, five years later sitting at a bistro table in his newly opened bakery, waiting for a mother and daughter to select a frosting color for a wedding cake. Soon he would no longer be a husband.

A couple came in the door with their arms around each other, and when they saw he was busy, found their way to the scrapbook with photos of wedding cakes. They began leafing through the photos and testimonials that all his paid and unpaid business advisors suggested were really important to starting out in the wedding cake business.

Right now, here at the table, the mother and her daughter had just agreed on the color of the frosting the young woman had chosen—celadon. Celadon sounded like a dinosaur he had read about as a kid, or a paint color he'd rejected when he and Jacqueline had argued about that, along with everything else, at the end. He remembered the color as celery green, green the color of fertility and of life.

Pale green. Not normal for a wedding cake but not unattractive, Mark thought. He preferred the white because the creamy confection had a goodness, and he felt white frosting would bode well for the future of the relationship. From his informal observations, it usually did, like a magic talisman, seem to make the wedding and the life after go smoothly. Or more smoothly.

Also, Mark had observed in his circle of friends and acquaintances that if people wrote their own vows, they were more likely to keep them. Some thought and feeling infused longevity into a relationship. Listening to a minister intoning the well-worn religious words that no one paid attention to anyway left too much time for day-dreaming and other distractions during these memorable moments.

Going over and over their troubles in his head, he had come to understand that there had been little buy-in on Jacqueline's part. They had vowed to partner in life, to share themselves spiritually, emotionally and physically and in a few other ways he had come up with to symbolize a real union of two people. And if part of what he had liked about her was her independent spirit, how could he have thought she would fit into the vision in his head of what a partner should be and do? Maybe it was the cake that was the mistake. Maybe the spice was wrong. Maybe he was right. A true compromise was to go with what the other person wanted, not suggest something completely different.

He remembered their cake, the compromise cake, spicy, layered with nutty filling and iced with a mocha-chocolate ganache. They had done a toast, eaten their meal, been toasted again and made their way from table to table talking and posing for photos and enjoying the assembly of friends and family they had created. Then the cake and the circus surrounding it. Family and guests poised with cameras, not to miss this moment. Mark not even getting a taste before the cake and ganache fell from his face to his suit jacket, to the floor. Jacqueline and all the female guests had been oddly triumphant.

Jacqueline was very self-sufficient, and she did not ask him for opinions. She had wanted to go back to school and ultimately did, to be an interior designer, a job where she could manipulate things better than people.

Throughout their marriage, they attended weddings of friends and family, and he began to wonder will this one last, thinking that each time he watched a bride on her father's arm, and saw the groom's rapt gaze. He began to speculate if pastors somehow kept tabs on the marriages and the divorces and did the math and came up with a percentage of pastoral success? And what number would be acceptable?

For a while he had thought that he and Jacqueline had something special. With the satisfaction of a man who had survived nearly five years of marriage, he would wonder who or what was at fault when hearing of friends or acquaintances calling it quits. Thinking about his own problems, he had begun to wonder if other separated or divorced people looked back to their pre-wedding days for a tip-off, that clue—if they hadn't been so blind in love— that might have influenced their decision.

And in the early part of his fifth year, his own marriage became a question after Jacqueline announced her intention to separate. All this had led him to own this storefront bakery in a marginal part of town, where he had quickly discovered the daily challenge of trying not to second-guess his wedding cake customers. Ironic, his choice of the bakery business—an avocation from college parlayed into a second career when Jacqueline complained about the long hours and the time apart that accompanied corporate life in a tough economy.

A spacious two-bedroom apartment upstairs was a fringe benefit of renting this storefront and the neighborhood was not so run-down that it would deter engaged couples from seeking him out. In the short time since the bakery had opened, his reputation for matching the cake with the ceremony, or the couple, was growing. The downside was that Jacqueline's apartment in a more upscale area was smaller and a number of her things still took up much of the space in his second bedroom. This meant sporadic and usually unannounced visits from her to collect this or that. It was irritating that when she stopped by, she behaved as though nothing were different, as though she hadn't suggested the separation several months earlier, that they hadn't disagreed about nearly everything. Mark thought about the many nights in the past few months that he had fallen asleep in the easy chair by the living room window, his last waking thought "what happened?"

When did things get so bad? How did they? He had been very involved with work, out a lot at night, missing dinners, working on speeches and annual reports, committee meetings to attend. Not a lot of attention for Jacqueline, who seemed to need more than either of them had thought. But Mark felt it went deeper than that, although he had never brought that up in the many exchanges that led to living in separate places. The more he thought about it, alone in his easy chair staring at the sunset, the more it seemed that there was trouble from the start, erupting for the first time at the cake table.

The couple was now looking at some cake samples, wedges in the glass-doored freezers that made up the wall to the left of the entrance. The man was lobbying for a cake with roses; the woman wanted daisies.

Roses were so common, she was saying, daisies were out of the ordinary. The man waxed romantic and talked about the sensuous curve of the petal, the meaningfulness of the colors, the red for passion, white for purity, yellow for friendship. He said it all meant something. That daisies were just white. She said that she felt they were putting too much importance on symbolism that didn't really exist.

Mark apologized for the wait and said that they would not find a cake with daisies in the shop.

The man shot his companion a triumphant glance.

Mark also said that didn't mean there could not be one.

The woman, clearly intrigued, said, "Really?"

Mark told them that from his perspective, cake baking and decoration was not rocket science, but it did take some imagination and a steady hand, both of which he brought to the table. The woman looked smug, the man doubtful.

Mark had seen the cake mean a lot of things—from the vicious to the sublime but chose not to add that to the discussion. He did offer that the cake was symbolic and quite meaningful. He explained that the cake was all about the bride. That in Victorian times, cakes were white, denoting purity and virginity. That the bride cuts the first piece with the groom's assistance, symbolizing the first task in the couple's life together. That the feeding of the cake to each other symbolizes their commitment to provide for each other. Of course, these days, he continued, it can turn into a pie-fight. Not smashing the cake is a trust issue. If you say it will not happen, you cannot, seized by the moment, smash the cake in your soul-mate's surprised and disappointed face.

The man and woman looked at each other, the man smug, the woman doubtful.

They sat down while he cut small pieces of several cakes and situated them on doilies on small china plates. The man tasted the chocolate with raspberry and mocha mousse filling and said "Wow" twice. He held out his fork to her. She shook her head and said she was thinking something fluffy and white.

Rich, chocolatey, and fruity. That's my style, the man said.

The woman said again that sweetness of a creamy, white cake would be more to her liking.

They asked about options for compromise.

Mark offered to make a ginger-spice cake that they could return to taste the next day. They agreed, the man looking forward to the symbolism and roses, the woman wanting tastiness and daisies. She left peeling imaginary petals from an imaginary flower and tossing them behind her chanting "he loves me, he loves me not." The man just smiled and shook his head.

Early that evening, Mark was adding the spices to the dry ingredients of the ginger-spice cake batter when he heard the bake shop doorbell chime. He had programmed the chime to be the first few bars of a favorite song, and it always made him smile. He grabbed a towel and was wiping his hands when Jacqueline walked into the kitchen.

"Just stopped in to pick up a few things," she said.

"Go ahead."

She walked toward the stairs and stopped at the bottom.

"You're all alone here." she said. "What could you possibly be smiling about?"

"This and that," he said, but was no longer smiling.

She went upstairs to his apartment and he heard her rooting around in boxes and closets.

He added the wet ingredients and grabbed a spatula for the blending.

Now maybe here was an opportunity.

Why did you do it? he would ask. Smearing cake in my face, when we had agreed none of that. Or was it just me? Was I the only one who agreed? It was a shock, Jacqueline. One I never really got over.

You are asking me this now? she might say. You've been wondering for nearly five years? This has been bothering you for that long? How could that not affect your thoughts about me, your trust in me?

Or maybe she might bring it up herself, smelling the spice cake, remembering. You are telling me this now? he would say slowly. For five years you've been keeping the reason for that breach of trust to yourself?

Jacqueline came down the stairs juggling two big boxes.

She stopped, leaning on the counter and inhaled, asked if it was spice cake.

He nodded and continued to mix the batter.

"I can smell it. I always loved that one. You know, when you were testing all your recipes, before, well before…"

"You mean before I spent a year reinventing myself as a baker trying to please you? Right before you said you didn't want to be together anymore no matter what?"

"Mark," she said, scooping her hair behind her ear.

He had heard her say his name that way before when she wanted to go to school for interior design and they could not afford it; when she preferred to delay starting a family at the point he had wanted to start trying; when they went to Aruba on vacation instead of to England, his

136

choice; even to the point of selecting new kitchen cabinets, the ones she picked out that required custom installation, not the ones he could easily install. He saw himself wiping cake from his face.

He stopped stirring and shook his head.

He ignored her questioning look and watched as she picked up the boxes and stopped at the door, then struggled with both the door and the boxes.

"Compromise. Over-rated," he muttered as he poured the batter down the garbage disposal, the fragrance of ginger, cinnamon and cloves wafting up from the drain.

"What'd you say?" she asked, just before the door closed behind her, the first few bars of the favorite song echoing in the approaching darkness.

Rice, Wild Rice

Geoff's mother thought that it was because of exposure to the lawn chemicals she had so zealously ordered each year at his father's request. His sister thought it was because he'd been a nerd and a geek all his life anyway. His friends thought it was because at his advanced age of twenty-eight, most of the gray cells were alcohol-laden and atrophied well before their time. Mindy thought it was because she knew him too well and he couldn't accept that. It was either that or something else that made him leave her standing at the altar.

Geoff wasn't really certain why he'd done it. He just knew that putting on the tuxedo had made his left eye twitch, pulling up in front of the church had caused a cold sweat, seeing Mindy so beautiful, sparkling in white and radiant with happiness, had made him tremble from the inside out. He had trembled to the point where his feet began to move. They turned him away from the minister, and from Gordy, his best man. They led him away from Mindy and pointed him to the secret door of escape into the small room, the one the minister sneaked through at some point during every service, either for prayer, inspiration or a cigarette, one could never be certain.

As Geoff stood in that small room, the innermost of sanctums, breathing through his nose and exhaling through his mouth like Mindy had told him she would eventually do in the throes of childbirth, he felt sure it wouldn't work. One woman forever seemed suddenly more like a punishment than a gift—even Mindy, his best friend, lover, so sweet and sour and tough and soft, so down-to-earth and yet so hard to understand. She was too much, he was sorry to say and it would take a while before he was equal to it. He could get there, he felt, but not that day, not in that suit, not at that church.

As the trembling abated, he began to think about the people waiting for him out there. They were clearing their throats about now, whispering with raised eyebrows. Mindy, in all her unflappability was probably flappable now, her deep green eyes maybe glistening with tears. She might even swoon and he hoped Gordy would be there to catch her as he had caught some of Geoff's miscalculations in the past.

He'd heard later there had been one hell of a scene, emotions ranging from indignation to embarrassment, from sighing to crying, some I-told-you-sos, and at least one wait-till-I-get-ahold-of-him. Gordy had told him that the men reacted less, said little, and shrugged their shoulders. Gordy had said that he thought some of them wished they had done the same many years earlier, wishes they would never dare share now.

And so, Geoff had slipped out the side door of the huge cathedral, removing his tie and suit coat with Superman-like panache, trying to blend into the midday crowd in a dress shirt and tuxedo trousers. He stopped to ask the limousine driver to step inside and tell the ushers he was gone. The driver nonchalantly handed him the bag of white rice Mindy had provided with instructions to toss on command, not too close to the church or to the car as rice was a mess to pick up.

It had all started with rice, that clump of white rice that Mindy presented proudly on that spring day, that first time she cooked for him. She had proclaimed it her Norwegian attempt at Chinese, chicken sliced thin, stir-fried with water chestnuts, onions, and something else that made the sauce all white, white and creamy like many Scandinavian entrees. All that on top of the sticky clumped-together white rice looked just too pale to Geoff, accustomed to the colorful sauces and spicier fare that his mother created effortlessly, seemingly in no time. Mindy had agonized over this meal and added all the appropriate spices and it smelled passably like Chinese. The open window in her tiny kitchen admitted a breeze that helped waft the fragrances of the simmering meal toward them, surrounding them eventually with the comfort of the first home-cooked meal they would share.

The table was set, right down to the plum wine and chopsticks, and they began to eat after the usual hungry welcoming kisses they both looked forward to. In fact, Geoff was hungrier for Mindy than for the food, but she led him to the table and dished out too many white foodstuffs for him not to make a comment. He had started gently, asking why there was no color in the food, no green color to be exact, no green onions or broccoli or even the light green of Chinese cabbage. She had replied that color was unnecessary, that taste should stand on its own. This resulted in a discussion of the art of cooking that grew more passionate as it grew longer.

Wasn't green the color of fertility? Shouldn't cooking be an expression of life? He began with these questions, all the while taking larger and larger bites of the chicken dish, which was actually not that bad. At first she wasn't hurt by his indirect criticisms, but a few more comments and he could see she was getting irritated. Then, when he tried to change the subject, she wouldn't let him, asking him what he would have done differently to this meal. Geoff, having culinary knowledge based only on what he liked to eat, not how to prepare it, and being utterly dependent on what little he might remember from the ladies' magazines he'd read in dentists' offices, replied perhaps some wild rice.

Mindy had gotten up from her seat opposite him then and grabbed a clump of the cooling congealing white rice from the oriental bowl she had bought just that afternoon to complement this meal. She stood next to him for a few seconds, then rubbed the rice purposefully on his face. Much of it stuck there, on his lips, in his nostrils, a few grains on his eyelids, some on his curly brown hair. For a moment he imagined her covered with a retaliatory clump, rice on her pouty lips, in her blonde Viking princess hair, around her green-as-the-deep-fjord eyes. Then he'd laughed. He'd liked it that she hadn't been afraid of her action, that she'd stood there, sticky hand on her hip, the rice starch a white smear on her sleeveless black dress, her entire body defiant and ready for whatever came next.

What came next was Geoff reaching for a handful of white ammunition. He stood up to full height next to her, and he was four inches taller, and she didn't flinch. He rubbed the rice on her shoulders and on her neck and began to eat it, the taste of the rice now mingling with the taste of her perfume, and of her. Some grains fell under the deep-cut neckline of her dress and watching her eyes, he searched for them with his fingers. He found them and she moved her sticky hand to his neck and rubbed it in his hair. Her tongue licked the rice from his lips and she moved toward the futon tucked conveniently in the corner as he reached for the bowl of this now welcome entree. He smeared rice on her lips and ate it from there, rubbed it on her breasts and tasted there. They continued to smear and taste until the rice was gone and the feeling of disconnectedness over it had long ago disappeared. This had been the first time they had made love, but not the last, and not the last involving food. A woman like this was worth a try, he remembered thinking as they lay side by side.

So, after about a year of meals, he had proposed, in spite of the occasional tastelessness of the food she diligently prepared, the lack of color, the dearth of spices, the vegetables underdone or overcooked, the meats never quite right. But she tried so hard, totally on her own, not having been taught the importance of food preparation, the techniques for fixing it not having been emphasized by anyone in her family. In this sense, having to blaze a trail alone, she was a pioneer woman, mastering the food processor, overcoming the stubbornness of the pasta machine, vanquishing the whimsy of the coffee maker, becoming one with the electric wok, overriding the years when she had lacked the opportunity to chop, slice, braise, dice, blanch or even sauté.

But a wedding ceremony didn't seem right for what they shared. He had told her this several times, wanting to wait just a little longer to extend this forever promise. But she had waited long enough, she said, several times, too, and it was her threat of moving on that made him take action. After the obligatory months of planning, on the appointed day, he had gone to the church early and alone, before anyone else, with loose white rice jiggling in his pocket to calm him, to make him remember what this was all about. But on that day, as he arrived and walked alone into the empty church all decorated with white roses and baby's breath tied with white satin bows, he visualized Mindy, all in white standing next to him in front of the minister in his white robe. He remembered the lackluster chicken soaking in the white sauce much more than he recalled the clumps of rice and what resulted. It all seemed just too bland. Yet later, waiting at the altar with Gordy and the minister, he thought he could get by that, trying in every way to forget all the whiteness that accompanied thoughts of Mindy. He visualized dinner at his parents' house, but those memories were filled with action and color, the deep green of romaine lettuce, the rich red of tomato sauce covering multicolored pasta, the cool yellow of the butter uniting the soft white inside and dark brown crust of his mother's homemade baguettes. Laughter and joy were in those colors. And excitement. That's when his feet had begun to move.

After causing the havoc at church, he walked around the city all day. He called Mindy when he got home and haltingly tried to invite himself over and failing that, to more articulately explain his desire to wait just a little longer. Although her silence on the other end was deadly, he told her everything, all his feelings right down to the intended effect of the white rice in his pocket. All this took many quarters from the pay phone near the church and he had to endure much honking from teenage girls cruising the strip delighted at seeing a handsome young man in a tuxedo filling a pay phone with coins. Eventually, through tears, she said she still couldn't understand. But she could give him some time, although she would not set the wheels in motion for a wedding again. He would have to do it and she may or may not be available. She slammed the phone and he could see her there, defiant, with her hand on her hip, ready for whatever came next.

After one month of extreme loneliness without her, and lots of thinking about her pioneer spirit, her not-always-successful culinary risks and daring combined with her sweetness, he called her. She invited him for dinner, which they ate while they discussed problems, reservations, sleeplessness—all his. She told him that even after everything, she still loved him and couldn't see her life without him.

And now, six months later, here he was again at the church, walking toward the steep marble front steps, again barely able to breathe, left eye twitching, bathed in a cold sweat, approaching the same limousine driver who looked at him, not nonchalantly this time, but with the shock of recognition. The driver apprehensively reached inside his jacket and handed Geoff the bag full of rice Mindy had once again provided. Geoff started to pocket the bag when he realized it had a different texture and looked to see that it contained white and brown grains with green flecks and a sandy-brown powder. He opened the small plastic bag and savored the pungent aroma of the mix. He looked up toward the double oak doors of the cathedral and saw that where previously white roses and baby's breath had decorated the banisters and entryway, now hung cornucopias overflowing with green and yellow and orange and red fruits and vegetables trimmed with equally colorful satin ribbon.

Now the fall breeze was invigorating as he strode up the marble steps toward the red carpet, as he saw Mindy again pioneering, her slender arms and delicate hands purposefully replacing the white rice in the bags with wild rice, a symbol of the journey they were beginning—tossed, spiced and mixed. As he opened the big oak door, he once again inhaled the fragrance of the bag's contents, and he recognized the perfume of commitment he knew they both could share—now that his eye had stopped twitching, now that he could breathe, now that he too was ready for whatever came next.

Fennel

I t wasn't the fault of those pots and pans she might leave simmering once in a blue moon on the stovetop. Marianne knew that it wasn't because it had all happened while they were gone, visiting his brother and his brother's kids two hours away, and she would never have left anything to simmer that long unsupervised, not even in a crockpot.

They could actually have gotten home sooner if the World Cup soccer game hadn't erupted into overtime, and then the win was so astonishing that everyone just had to experience the post-game show. They had watched the female sports commentator stride nonchalantly into the locker room, eyes roaming, examining the well-honed and sculpted soccer player bodies for the ones she most wanted to interview. They'd watched the players, exuberant from the win, squirt each other and everyone else with champagne. They'd seen the players hesitate ever so briefly, weighing the consequences of including the woman in their revels. Then the spirit of the win seized the players once again and she was decked out not just in a black suit and off-white silk blouse, but also in champagne, shaken, not stirred, and shaken again before it exploded, released by players who would much rather wear it than drink it.

They watched the presentation of the trophy, but Marianne was riveted more closely to her watch as it became six-thirty and then seven.

"We'd best get going," she said several times in several different ways.

Once, they actually all got up, her Irishman, his brother, his brother's kids—all men without a woman's sensibilities and sensibleness, not anticipating the workday of tomorrow coming all too soon. But then came the highlights, and wanting to relive in slow motion what they had seen only as a blur during the actual game forced them back into their chairs, with no attention paid to her stiff frame standing in the doorway.

The Irishman finally caught her eye and her breath stopped again at his glance, the years of passion, of the "troubles" seared into his eyes, making the iris as dark as the pupil, the way of understanding him as big a secret now as it was a year ago when their casual meeting heated into so much more.

"You're thinking about tomorrow, aren't you, darlin'," he brogued, limping across the room to massage her very tense neck. He tossed back the shock of black hair that covered his forehead and often at least one eye. He reached under her chestnut, wavy hair and began a rhythmic motion with his thumbs.

"You're always thinking about that," he said. He wasn't tall and the leg with the bullet hole scar made one side of him even shorter. Physical therapy was helping now, a miracle so many years after the injury, and the limp was less pronounced, and his ego less fragile. The "troubles" would always take their toll, he would say to anyone interested, gesturing down. He fancied himself a tragic Hemingway character, only with a different wound, thank God, because impotence was not something he could bear, and didn't have to.

"Sean, I'll see you," her Irishman had whispered to his brother, not wanting to distract him too much from the remains of the post-game. Sean waved good-bye, glued to the near movie-sized monitor displaying the vestiges of the day's triumph, glued to the winning coach's words about loyalty and team spirit and self-sacrifice.

In the darkness of the car he asked if she would make him something special when they got home, something in celebration of the win, something that was as sweet and courageous and tantalizing as she was. She wondered out loud what that could be. It was an innocent wondering but a hopeful one, hoping that he would say he was kidding so she could get ready for bed and watch the beginning of that Ingmar Bergman film like she used to, when things were less complex. When she summoned her strongest voice to question his seriousness, because with her Irishman it was sometimes hard to tell, he shrugged and she thought he was probably wondering why she even asked.

He was always serious about food, the one thing she had no sense of humor about either. Their mealtimes were silent except for comments on taste and smell and spice, with the possible exception of the nights when the six o'clock news went to Ireland for reasons, good or bad, that usually became apparent right after the next commercial. They savored what she created, always easy on the spices now, for as the Irishman was fond of saying, "Passion is the spice of life. Why use additives?"

On this night, scones came to mind because she had a mix and his late night snack could be quick and dirty. With a cup of tea—and she would try to slip him decaf—this might be just the relaxing foodstuffs he needed.

"Not scones," he said, not knowing he was reading her mind once again. "Something we can share against the pillows as we read our Bible verses tonight."

And in the darkness of the car, she sensed his magical wink, and even now at the end of a tiring day, it raised her body temperature two or three degrees. It contained everything it had needed to grab her attention: a sense of humor, a love of life, and a flirtatious promise that she couldn't forget for days after she had first seen him at her book signing.

*****

On that day, he'd waited in line for a long time and when he reached her, he had not asked her to autograph her latest cookbook triumph, her reason for being in downtown Boston in the first place. Instead, he'd shoved forward a book of contemporary Irish poems for her to sign. When she'd protested, he'd winked and flipped the book open to what seemed to be a familiar page, then began to read, his husky and earnest voice caressing the words and infusing them with life. The people in the bookstore that day, Marianne thought now, probably would have given anything to be with him, sit enraptured by his colorful stories, donate money for the troubles at home, at the very least treat him to a brew at the local pub. Many might have wanted to reach into his mind to grab some of his passion for themselves, emotion they could use as an ace in the hole when their everydays were just too boring, too black and white, too lacking. If only we were Irish, she had sensed men thinking as he read his poem. If only he were mine, she had seen those wishes in the shining eyes of every women standing in line, I'd make him forget.

In an irony greater than the ones she sprinkled liberally throughout the short stories she sometimes wrote, at first she hadn't even been interested, thought him a boor, and too short at that. He was stealing her time to shine. It was **her** book-signing, **her** public reading, **her** dinner out with the bookstore owners, who, also beguiled, begged him to join them. They had been seated in the dimmest corner of the restaurant, at his request, in a swanky booth with Moroccan leather seats, hand-dipped beeswax candles, linen napkins edged with Irish lace, the type his grandmother, God rest her soul, had created in the evenings as she spun tall tales before the fire. He charmed and entertained effortlessly, she'd had to admit to herself, with a touch here, a whisper and a wink there, and he was so solicitous of her. They were—she was—in his spell. Observing the way that he had of massaging egos, he'd soon ask for a signed cookbook, she was sure.

At the door of her hotel suite that night, she waited for that ask, but it didn't come. She was disappointed by that as well as by no motion toward the kiss she'd expected from that very self-assured man. Marianne unlocked her door and turned to shake his hand, which he had ready, and then she slipped inside to endure the night, sleepless and wondering about the unpredictability of a man who spent the evening with his knee pressuring hers under the table, with his eyes never leaving hers, even when he was entertaining their group of six, making her feel like they were two people alone, about to make a dangerous connection.

Marianne answered the hotel room door the next morning, expecting room service and finding the Irishman, with two giant coffees and croissants, with circles under his eyes from sharing his night with her in his head and heart, he said. This he told her again much later, after she had invited him inside. And how could she not after he set their breakfast down on the hall table, took her hands in his and pleaded for her to release his heart. Playfully, she had murmured she couldn't, but the playing stopped when he reached for her and rubbed his middle finger a little beneath her collarbone and whispered that then he must surely have her heart as well. Everything got serious then.

Marianne, without a thought for good sense, the sense for which she was famous in her family, dropped her guard, for which she was also famous, only in a wider circle, and gave him the kiss he said he would have taken the night before, were it not for the uncertain look in her eyes. The kiss lasted as long as it took to cook a three-minute egg, long enough to make them both breathless and wanting more. Over cold coffee and croissants, amid clothes strewn here and there, she first saw the place where the bullet went in. She gently massaged the tightened skin and her tears fell on the scarred surface of his leg as he told her the story of it all. Never, she thought, never have I met a man like this one.

It was a week or so later that she remembered to ask about the book of poems, that particular poem that had so affected the crowd that night in the bookstore. He reluctantly produced it from the inside pocket of his army green trench coat and she saw it was his, his book, with his name, containing his poems, and she couldn't believe how stupid she was for not having seen it, for having been blinded by seven days of passion and sensual discovery, during which he had kept this one secret from her. Why wouldn't a poet want his woman to know, she had asked. It was awkward, he had said, a poet seducing a cookbook writer, like a muse trying to get inside the head of a chef, from one who takes nothing literally to one who takes nothing for granted. Even in this explanation, where she

152

should have learned volumes, she was so carefully measuring the ingredients of their relationship that she learned only what she wanted, so that it would have the all-important heat it needed to keep rising.

*****

As they approached their neighborhood at the end of the two-hour ride, the sky burned red. There was commotion, too, bells clanging and sirens wailing, all converging on her small house, all meeting there too late to save anything. For once his glib Irish tongue waxed silent as he held her, both of them trembling before the smoke and flame billowing from her kitchen window.

In the cleanup days following, she found that not a recipe, not a cookbook had survived. All the times she'd not committed a recipe to memory because she would always have the cookbook, were now a mockery. Irreplaceable losses in the form of charred photographs of those she loved overwhelmed her. No photos—not even the one of her mother and father as bride and groom—still existed. And her short story collections, their publication so laboriously won, destroyed. Had the oven been left on, still containing remains of the previous night's vegetarian offering, another trial for a new collection of meatless recipes? These things she wondered, fearing she might have caused her own personal catastrophe. She didn't remember, although it would have been unusual for her to forget any kind of food in mid-preparation, at least until the Irishman.

From the night of the inferno that was her small home, she had sensed a difference. It was subtle, but it was definitely a blaming. She'd been making a chicken stew to bring to his brother's that day, one with many ingredients, and, even though he said he loved her culinary creativity, he'd teased her for the meticulous way she was preparing the dish. She'd teased him back for his focus on soccer and he had wanted her right then but, seeing her very focused on the creating, had tried to distract her with touches and tiny kisses, and it had worked as always. And then she'd nearly forgotten to bring the dish, remembered it only after half an hour of the drive had passed and then only because she was thinking about their time together that afternoon, and what she'd been doing before they ended up snuggled in her bed under the thick European-style feather comforter he'd bought her. They'd gone back for it and he'd asked then if she had turned off the oven, and she'd said she had, certain of it, remembered the clicking sound as she did it, remembered leaving the casserole dish in there just to keep it warm while they got ready. She'd asked him about the cigar, the one he'd lit in the living room while she was still getting dressed, the one he never could smoke without a finger of whiskey. He said he'd ground it out, remembered the scratching sound it made against the side of the ashtray, remembered balancing it on the side to light up again later. So who was to blame then, if indeed someone had forgotten something, she wondered, the seducer or the seducee?

As she sat down with the insurance adjuster she realized that, like the language of insurance policies, many other things had become ambiguous to her since the Irishman. The fire investigators couldn't trace the blaze to any negligence, thank God for this big favor. And she herself had gotten over the nagging feeling that the blaze was her fault. The only one who was hounded by that was the poet. And probably that was because his volume of poems had perished as well. In the months following "the destruction" as she called it privately to herself, he became less poetic, less energetic.

He became a heavy weight in her rented, fully furnished apartment where they lived while the construction company rebuilt her home. He moped about his poetry book, scorched beyond recognition. He whined when he could not find the right word for a new stanza, and blamed his lack of creativity on the fire, flames having a well-known knack for feeding on oxygen, the very element he needed to be able to breathe, and to create. The flames that had made them cling together in horror had sucked the life from the Irishman, sucked away his creativity, romance, and not to belabor the point, his passion. How had he ever endured "the troubles," Marianne thought to herself, if he can't endure the loss of a single volume of poems. She'd lost it all. Her recipes would never be the same. Her family would have to exist now only in her memory until a new camera would help make the present the immediate past. Her life existed only from the moment of "the destruction" forward. He still had the scar and all the unwritten poems that flowed, although not smoothly and certainly not gently, from his hand to the pen to the paper.

*****

Pans steaming on the stove, lids clattering amidst the boiling demanded her attention as she sat semi-reclined on the cushions of the window seat in the dining room of her new bungalow. Checking those in a minute would be a good thing, she knew, especially the asparagus which she was steaming without much water as it was. But there were just a few more pages to read and it was such a gripping tale and surely vegetables could wait on the completion of a good read, especially if the words she was reading were her own.

She loved rereading the new stories she had written. It was like attending a high school reunion where forgotten strong feelings for old friends and acquaintances powerfully resurfaced. These stories evoked emotions, some long buried, bubbling like the asparagus waiting for attention.

Her thumb marked the spot in the notebook where she'd stopped reading. The notebook slipped into her lap just as her attention skittered back across several months to warmer weather and, she had thought, better times when she was still cooking for two. Then she would have been perched on the stool in the kitchen, one eye monitoring her charges; the perfectly matched pots and pans full of lovingly peeled potatoes, julienned carrots, grated cabbage and corned beef steeped for days in just the right spices to make just the right impression on her Irishman. Opening the oven door would have emitted the delicate scent of Irish soda bread containing just the right amount of raisins and a little less caraway than the recipe called for because caraway was not his favorite. She couldn't leave it out, she had felt, because then it wouldn't be soda bread, not really.

But caraway wasn't a subtle flavor and he had discerned right away her stubborn adherence to the recipe, her inflexibility another brick in the growing wall between them. His increasing criticism of her culinary skills irritated her even more than his after dinner cigar and several whiskeys; his avowed need for relaxation had become her allergy attack.

She thought again about that evening several weeks ago and the sausage links she'd created literally from conception, buying hog intestines for skins, grinding several meats together innumerable times with a hand

156

grinder attached to the table. She'd ground the meat to the point of severe elbow pain, so vigorous was her motion. The meat was so smooth that it had a melt-in-your-mouth consistency, literally no gristle. And when it was set to spice, she'd paused with the fennel poised to sprinkle lightly, but some devilish whim bubbled forth and the sprinkling became a dumping. The fennel permeated not only the meat mixture but the kitchen as well as she mixed the meat with her hands just the way the ethnic cookbook advised.

He hadn't even tasted it before he left in a typhoon of Irish invective, citing once again her inability to please him in oh so many ways. He stormed out in a self-righteous huff, with God or someone on his side, packing furiously and lightly, though with great panache, ties and a shirtsleeve pinched in the edges of his angry suitcase.

And in his poet's heart, he probably thought that all this hurt, that he had precipitated this final trouble with his displeasure for her. In his haste to escape, he couldn't have read her mind one more time. He couldn't have known that as thankful as she had been for the infusion of adrenaline that accompanied him a year ago, now she anticipated the peace and quiet his absence would afford.

She opened her notebook again, and a fennel seed peered forth from the spine. Dear, dear seed, she thought. The spice that broke the camel's back. Unfolding herself from the comfort of the cushions, she glided serenely across the dining room into the kitchen. She poked a fork into the perfect asparagus and sighed with pleasure, glancing gratefully at her bulging spice rack, the empty fennel jar alone in the place of honor, a trophy high on the top shelf, a permanent reminder of the value of additives.

About the Author

Kathy Johncox was born in St. Louis, Missouri but gathered material and developed story ideas in seven states and two countries before settling down to write them at her current home in upstate New York. Her fiction has been published in print in *Buffalo Spree Magazine, Lake Affect Magazine* and *The New England Writers' Network,* and online in *Inkburns, an Online Literary Journal* and in *Potpourri: A Magazine of the Literary Arts.*

www.kathyjohncoxbooks.com

Made in the USA
Charleston, SC
11 November 2012